The Jacket

Meredith Kennedy

Strategic Book Group

Copyright 2011
All rights reserved — Meredith Kennedy

No part of this book may be reproduced or transmitted in any form or by any means, graphic, electronic, or mechanical, including photocopying, recording, taping, or by any information storage retrieval system, without the permission, in writing, from the publisher.

Strategic Book Group
P.O. Box 333
Durham CT 06422
www.StrategicBookClub.com

ISBN: 978-1-60911-183-0

Printed in the United States of America

To DD and David, who are always looking deeper and farther into what makes us human.

DAY ONE

The sound of breaking glass suddenly emanated from the pocket of Jax's baggy jeans. Wiping his sticky fingers on the seat of his pants, he casually dug his cell phone out of his pocket and flipped it open. The breaking glass ringtone drove his mother nuts, but somehow he just hadn't gotten around to changing it to something else. The caller ID on his phone read 'BOOGERHEAD'—his affectionately chosen nickname for Karen, his next-door neighbor and friend since they were four years old. When he called her phone, 'SCUMBUCKET' showed up on her screen. Their birthdays were within a week of each other, and they had been best friends for the past twelve years.

"Hey, dudette," Jax said into the phone. He'd forgotten his Bluetooth upstairs in his room.

"Jax: the man, the mystery, the legend," replied Karen. "How are you?"

"What do you want now?" he asked, pretending to be annoyed. He bit into his snack and crunched noisily into the phone.

"Oh, *God*. Jax, please don't tell me you're eating one of those big smelly pickles!" Karen complained.

Jax grinned. He could picture her making a face—her freckled nose scrunching up and scowling behind her horn-rimmed glasses. "Okay," he replied, "I won't." *Crunch. Smack. Gulp.*

"…And don't tell me you've doused it with cayenne pepper, for crying out loud!" she groaned.

Jax let her savor the sounds of his chewing for a moment before responding. "It enhances my pickle-eating experience."

"*Ugh*. I can smell the garlic from here," Karen replied.

"Was there something you wanted?" Jax asked her. "Or did you just call to listen to me eat?" He smacked his lips noisily.

"No, actually, I didn't call for that," she said. "But if I ever hear the toilet flush when I'm talking to you, I'm *never* calling you again."

"Promise?" Jax grinned. He tried balancing his phone between his chin and shoulder.

Karen let out an exasperated sigh. "Listen, doofus-head. I'm at the mall with Connor and Celeste, and we ran into Andy and Simone. Anyway, we found the coolest jacket. It's red leather—kind of a bomber jacket—with these really cool silver snaps up the front. It's sort of a dark red; my mom would call it ox-blood or something weird like that," she explained excitedly. "It's at Vintage Collectibles. Honestly, it's *awesome*."

"And this pertains to me how, exactly?" Jax wondered. *Crunch.*

"We're forming a consortium! A clothing co-op!" Karen exclaimed. Jax could hear the excitement in her voice. When she got like this, her hazel eyes grew wide behind her thick glasses. She wasn't exactly beautiful, but her face had a way of lighting up that he always found endearing—pretty even.

Karen continued. "It's too expensive for one or two people to buy, but if there are six of us, we each only have to pay sixty-two dollars and forty-seven cents. That's including tax."

Jax still didn't understand what she wanted from him. "And you want me to…do what, exactly?"

"Buy into the consortium, doofus-face! We need a sixth person!" she cried.

"Well, I'm sure I'm much more likely to cooperate if you keep calling me names," he joked.

"Oh, *whatever*. Listen, I can front the money since I'm here, and you can pay me back," Karen said quickly. "Simone has an extra padlock we can use for an empty locker at school; we're planning to keep the jacket there. Then we'll make a schedule for who's wearing it when."

Jax sighed. "A red jacket?" he asked doubtfully. "Do I look like a red jacket kind of guy?"

"Oh, come on, Jax! It's understated and tasteful. It's a cool red jacket. Besides, Andy thinks it's cool. Don't you, Andy?" she asked. Jax could hear other voices in the background.

"Andy, the *football player,* thinks it's cool?" Jax replied incredulously. "Put him on the phone."

There was a moment of random noise and then Andy spoke into Karen's phone. "What's up, dude?"

"Yo, man. What's with the jacket?" Jax asked him.

"It's okay, dude. It's kind of cool," Andy replied.

"Am I gonna look like a complete lunchbox wearing this thing?" Jax wanted to know.

"No, man, it's okay. I mean, the chicks like it…"

"Oh," Jax laughed. "Well, say no more then."

"Later, man," Andy said. He handed the phone back to Karen. It was the longest conversation he had ever had with Hillman High School's star quarterback. Jax suspected it was about the longest conversation Andy ever had with anyone, including Simone, his girlfriend.

"Well, you in, or what?" Karen demanded. She seemed to be growing impatient "Don't you want to be one of the cool people?"

"I already *am* one of the cool people. I should be asking *you* that." He could practically see Karen making a face again. "Yeah, I'm in. I'll pay you back." An idea was crystallizing in the back of his mind. *Maybe this jacket would make him look older, taller, and more sophisticated. Maybe he would look cool enough to be taken seriously at an audition—someone who would be a real asset to a band, and not just a gawky sixteen-year-old kid who likes music. Maybe he could be someone different in this jacket…*

"Great! I'll meet you at school tomorrow. You can see the jacket then. You're gonna *love* it," Karen gushed breathlessly. Jax smiled; his buddy was unstoppable when she got her teeth into something.

"I have an audition this Saturday at 8:00 P.M. Sign me up for the jacket then, okay?" he asked.

"Oh, Jax! With Seventh Heaven?" Karen exclaimed. "Congratulations!"

"Yup. Got a call this morning. They're going to hear me sing and play guitar, and they said I can play a couple of my own pieces." Jax couldn't keep the grin from his face. He could already imagine himself with the band, onstage playing guitar—an electric guitar (which he didn't have yet)—with cool shades and now a red leather jacket.

"That's awesome! I can't believe it has taken them this long to get back to you. They *better* take you!" Karen said dramatically. She was his biggest fan. She laughed, adding, "Well, I'm sure they will when they hear your songs, but at least you'll be looking hot in the new jacket!"

§ § § § §

"Celeste, will you please hand me that roll of tape?" Karen stretched out one hand while she used the other to hold the flaps of a cardboard box together. She was president of the Bookworms Literary Society, and it was sponsoring a book drive at school. Posters had been up for a week, urging classmates and teachers to bring in books that the group would then donate to schools in developing countries.

"Tell me again how you know this school in Belize," Celeste said as she gave Karen the roll of wide brown tape. The books collected in the drive were to be packaged up and mailed to a school there.

Celeste Nguyen and Karen Little couldn't have been more different: Celeste was petite and Asian, with short, glossy black hair and an elfin face; Karen was tall and gangly, about twenty pounds overweight, with wavy, unruly reddish-brown hair, and glasses. She kept her hair tied back in a ponytail, but it stubbornly refused to stay put, with renegade wisps and curls that framed her freckled face and glasses. Karen envied Celeste for her beautiful, sleek black hair, which barely brushed her shoulders and always looked perfect. As Celeste turned toward Karen, her hair gently swung in a single shining sheet. Karen's heart sighed—*If only I had such beautiful hair. Maybe it would be if I got it straightened. Perhaps if it weren't such a dull brown...Chestnut! Remember, it's chestnut, not brown...*

"It's through my family doctor," said Karen, snapping to. "She's been to Belize twice, doing free clinics and taking donated medicines and supplies with her. She made friends with the headmaster of the school in this little village, and they need books for the kids. Here, put your hand here." *How does Celeste get such a gorgeous complexion? She has the most beautiful smooth skin, and I have a bunch of random zits and freckles. I wish I were Asian...*

Celeste followed instructions and held the flaps of the box in place while Karen taped it. The girls quietly assembled boxes for a few minutes until Celeste suddenly remembered the red jacket.

"So, how excited you are about Friday night?" she asked with a grin.

Karen looked up from one of the boxes. "Oh, yeah!" she beamed. "I'll be the first official wearer of the red jacket at Melina's birthday bash. You should see this amazing little black skirt I'm gonna wear with it."

"Yeah? What does your mom think?" Celeste knew that Karen and her divorced mother didn't always see eye to eye about things like clothes, attending church (her mother did; Karen didn't), and dating. Karen was already making plans for how she was going to get the skirt, the jacket, and the stiletto heels out of the house without her mom seeing.

"What my mom doesn't know won't hurt her," Karen shrugged. "She's not gonna see the red jacket, either. I'm going with Simone and Andy, and they're bringing it in Andy's car. I'll be changing once we get there."

"You've got it all planned out!" Celeste laughed. "Oh, David's gonna be there, too, isn't he?"

Karen's hazel eyes sparkled behind her glasses as she smiled her crooked smile. She felt her face flush with embarrassment. David Steinberg was the big reason Karen had been quick to sign up for the red jacket for Friday night. She had spoken to David exactly three times in her life; she doubted he even knew her name. But Friday night he would know Tess…

Tess Tramontine was the other big reason Karen needed the red jacket for Friday night's party. Tess Tramontine was Karen's *nom de plume*—the name she'd chosen for herself when she'd decided she was going to become a journalist: *This is Tess Tramontine, reporting live from the refugee camp in Boca Raton, where a deadly new strain of the Bobulus-Marconi virus has been discovered.*

Karen was ordinary, plump, gawky, and clumsy—the schoolmarmish president of the Bookworms. Tess, on the other hand, was confident, leggy, and sleek—a sophisticated professional who had been on so many international flights she'd lost count. Tess would fly into remote third world locations covering the stories of brave women trying to raise their families in guerilla war zones, and then she'd attend cocktail parties in Paris, hobnobbing with celebrities and executives, charming them into donating money to relief organizations.

If Karen were going to Melina's birthday party, she would show up wearing thick glasses; Tess would wear contacts (disposable lenses borrowed from a friend). Karen would wear faded corduroy pants and sensible shoes; Tess would wear a stretch black skirt and red spike heels (borrowed from another friend). Karen would wear tiny studs in her pierced ears; Tess would be wearing glittering, dangly gold-and-red earrings bought secretly at an art fair last summer (and saved for this occasion).

On Friday night, Tess Tramontine would be making her debut at Melina's party. No parents would be present, and the red jacket would make her complete. David had never noticed Karen before, but he *had* to notice Tess.

"Hey, Connor!" Celeste called out. Karen immediately stopped daydreaming again as Connor approached the book club table with a large grocery bag filled with books.

"Our first books!" Karen exclaimed excitedly. Connor set the bag down and smiled proudly. "You rock, Connor." She peered inside the bag. "Are these all your Danielle Steele novels?"

"Very funny," replied Connor. He was tall and slender, with wavy dark blond hair and greenish-gray eyes. "My mom got them from her friend who teaches third grade." He pulled one of the books out of the bag. "See? *Fun with Numbers.* They're gonna love this in Belfast." His eyes danced. He was jerking Karen's chain.

"Uh huh," Karen replied. "Pop quiz! Where is Belize anyway, genius?"

"Right next to Guatemala, Central America—home of the Mayan empire," he said with a grin. "You think I'm a dumb blond, don't you?"

"No, I think you're a doofus," Karen smirked. "Anyway, thanks for the books." She started loading the donated books into one of the cardboard boxes.

"*Jax* is the doofus, remember?" Connor joked. He turned to Celeste and glanced at his watch. "Got your violin? Better hustle. Rehearsal is in twelve minutes." Celeste nodded and began packing up her belongings.

"Celeste, hold on," said Karen. "Just help me close up this box; the side keeps wanting to fall apart." Karen ripped another piece of packing tape from the roll, held it in her teeth, and grabbed Celeste's hand to hold it against the sagging box. "Hold that right there while I tape it shut. Thanks."

Karen's back was turned away as a guy in a blue hoodie happened to be walking by the table. Connor quickly waved him over. His eyes mischievous, he silently motioned to the newcomer to keep quiet as he grabbed his hand and placed it on the cardboard box in place of Celeste's hand.

Oblivious to what just happened, Karen started to stick the big piece of tape onto the box. She continued taping until she suddenly discovered that the large hand holding the flaps in place was not Celeste's. Startled, she turned her head to discover that David was now helping her out with the box.

"Oh!" she gasped. She could feel her heart start to flutter. "Um...I...uh..." She was in shock. She never expected in a million years that his face would be so close to hers. He was the most beautiful man she had ever seen, with sky-blue eyes, sandy light-brown hair, and a movie star smile. *Ohmigod! Of course I have to have a zit the size of a volcano on my chin, and why haven't I gotten contact lenses* yet? When did I last wash my hair? Did I put on deodorant this morning? I think I did. Are there bits of cornflakes in my teeth? Agh!*

David sensed her nervousness and grinned. "Hi, there," he said. His beautiful voice floated over her chunky glasses, spotty face, and messy hair. "I, uh, gotta get to class. Um, do you think you could...?" He glanced down at the box of books and Karen's eyes immediately followed. That's when she realized she had taped his hand directly onto the side of the box.

Horrified, she ripped the tape off, freeing David's hand and allowing the flimsy cardboard to sag again, letting the books start to slide out. "Oh, I'm—I'm so sorry...I didn't see..."

"No problem," he answered, smiling that unbelievable smile at her.

Ohmigod! He's smiling at me. I can't believe it! I wonder if I just ripped seven layers of skin off his poor hand. Karen glared over at Connor, who was stifling a laugh. Celeste just stood there, dumbfounded. She knew what a crush Karen had on David, and so she tried not to crack a smile over the silliness of the situation.

David gave a little wave and walked off down the hall, shifting his backpack up on his shoulder. Karen stared after him for a few moments, but she jumped when the sound of books hitting the floor shocked her back into reality. Quickly, she knelt and started gathering them up.

Tess Tramontine won't have cornflakes in her teeth. Tess never has zits and always smells beautiful and sexy. Once I've got that red jacket, Tess is going to really *get his attention. Just wait...*

§ § § § §

Celeste hurried to join Connor as they headed off to the orchestra room. "Slow down! Only one of us has mile-long legs here, and it's not me!"

"You going to Melina's party this Friday?" Connor wanted to know. It was the big event of the season. Word was getting around that there would be no parents. Even more importantly, Melina's big brother had agreed to provide alcohol.

Celeste sighed. "My mother found out that Melina's parents are away for the weekend," she muttered. "I'm not allowed to go."

Connor nodded sympathetically. He couldn't imagine having parents as strict as hers. She was not allowed to leave the house wearing wrinkled clothing; she had a 10:00 P.M. curfew every night; and she had to practice her violin for two hours every day—four hours a day on weekends. She was, of course, a straight-A student. Celeste's parents had great expectations when it came to their beloved daughter; she was to become a concert violinist. She had been made first violin and concertmaster of the Hillman High orchestra. She had even won several state and national music competitions.

In the orchestra room, Connor and Celeste sat together and rosined their bows. Although Celeste was national scholarship material when it came to music, Connor was no slouch. At sixteen years old, Connor was tall—about six feet tall and still growing—but, to his father's dismay, he wasn't into sports. He hated basketball. Football didn't interest him either. His father was senior partner in a large and prestigious law firm with his own expectations for his son. One day, he wanted Connor to follow in his footsteps and become a lawyer, too.

Celeste knew that Connor's father wanted him to go into law. She also knew Connor much better than his father seemed to. Connor had a sensitive personality, and he was a good listener; his father was loud and domineering. The adversarial life of an attorney didn't appeal to him since he was an artist and musician. He had aspirations of going to art school. Celeste had seen his sketchbooks, all filled with beautiful drawings, and knew he was already a talented artist. They'd spent many hours out walking in the woods behind Connor's house, or sitting on the rocks by the stream that meandered through them. Celeste knew a lot about Connor. In fact, she was the only person alive who knew his other secret.

"So, is tonight the night?" she asked him, doing her best to appear casual as she arranged her music on the music stand in front of her.

Connor shook his head. "No, my dad's out of town until next week. He got some call about a meeting and left yesterday morning."

"Are you going to tell your mom first?" Celeste treaded carefully.

"I don't think so. I really want to tell them together." A shadow crossed Connor's face—a slight frown furrowing the brow above his gray-green eyes. Celeste had seen this look so many times as they'd discussed his situation by the river, or while walking through the pines.

"I think I'll tell them next Wednesday," he told her with conviction. "That's when my dad comes back from his trip." They both knew he couldn't put it off any longer. It was with him day and night—the feeling that he was somehow deceiving his family by pretending to be someone he wasn't. *I have to give them a chance to know me and love me for who I really am, not as some impostor.* It was the mature thing to do. He wasn't a kid anymore.

"Well, call me and let me know how it goes," Celeste said to him, flipping through her sheet music. "Oh, wait! I'm going out on Wednesday night."

"You're *what?*" Connor stared at her in amazement. "Your parents are actually letting you out of the house?"

She grinned and shrugged her shoulders. "My aunt is setting me up with a Vietnamese boy she knows through her husband's relatives. He's in college, and he's coming to town next week. I'm only allowed to go out with him and his friends—past curfew!—and I'm sure we'll end up going out to a bingo game or something…"

Connor laughed and shook his head, playing. "Past curfew? Wahoo!" He wrapped a long arm around her slim shoulders. "Our little Celeste is growing up!"

Celeste leaned over conspiratorially. "I'll tell you what, though—I've signed out the red jacket for Wednesday night," she said in a hushed voice. "I don't care where we end up, but I intend to have a good time!"

DAY THREE

Simone held the red jacket up and grinned at Andy. She was six inches shorter than her boyfriend, with luminous brown eyes and long honey-blond hair. Normally she kept it tied back for cheerleading practice, but now it flowed in delightful disarray around her shoulders. Simone had taken the jacket from its locker at school to give to Karen when they picked her up for the party; Karen was scheduled to have it for tonight. But it was still early, and Simone and Andy had driven up to the water tower for a little rest and relaxation.

Being dyslexic, Andy had always had a hard time with academics. He had sat behind Simone in their English composition class. Staring at her soft honey hair had not helped his concentration, and by midterm he was receiving failing grades. Finally, he worked up the courage to ask Simone, a straight-A student, if she would help him study. With Simone's help, Andy ended up passing the English composition class with flying colors. They had been together ever since—a year and three months—and driving up to the water tower was a favorite pastime of theirs.

"Come *on,* Andy! I want to see it on you," she cajoled, holding the jacket out to him as they both leaned against the hood of Andy's dad's car. They had driven up to their favorite spot after their afternoon football and cheerleading practice.

"You *already* saw it on me," Andy told her. He playfully rolled his eyes and lit up a cigarette. They had all tried on the jacket at Vintage Collectibles when they'd first bought it two days ago. It had barely fit Andy, but he agreed to pitch in for it anyway. It hung down to midthigh on Simone, making her look like an adorable elf in dark red leather; only her fingertips showed at the ends of the sleeves. It had had the same effect with Celeste, who was also petite. Tall and gawky Karen had a statuesque air about her when she'd put it on.

Andy raised the cigarette to his lips again, but Simone deftly snatched it from him. "Hey!" he scowled, a little annoyed. He was afraid that she'd drop it, and it was his last one.

Simone laughed and cocked her head, causing her shaggy dark golden bangs to fall over one eye. She still couldn't believe it was him, Andy Greentree, right in front of her. He was the object of so many schoolgirl crushes; she'd thought he would never even be interested in her. But one day, to her amazement, he had asked her to help him with his homework. Simone wasn't a stereotypical cheerleader by any means. She was really interested in math and science. The only reason she'd managed to get on the squad was through her excellent gymnastic skills.

She'd been taking gymnastics since the age of seven, after having spent three months hospitalized with terrible seizures from which she nearly hadn't recovered. When she was finally able to go home, she was weak and debilitated and needed a year of physical therapy. Gymnastics had seemed like a good form of artistically-oriented rehabilitation. Simone's mother had worked hard at home-tutoring her so she wouldn't be behind the other kids in her class. Two years later, Celeste finally caught up to speed with her classmates. In fact, by then she was actually ahead of her peers in math, science, reading, and English. After lots of practice, she also became passably good in gymnastics. But she had never felt part of the 'in' crowd, or particularly popular. That's why when popular football star Andy took a liking to her, she almost couldn't believe it.

Simone tossed the red jacket at him with one hand and held the cigarette up in the air with the other. "No ciggie until you put the jacket on!" she teased, making the cigarette dance in her little fingers. Her velvet brown eyes crinkled at the edges when she grinned, and her short cheerleader costume flounced as she twirled. She hadn't yet changed for the party, which was fine with Andy because he *loved* the little white pleated skirt on her—especially when it didn't stay in place.

He could hardly refuse. He put the jacket on.

"Sugar!" Simone squealed. "You look *fiiiiiine*." The elegant bomber jacket barely fit over Andy's broad shoulders, but he couldn't quite get it to close in the front. He was six feet tall, with light brown hair and blue eyes, and a mole on the left side of his chin. When he'd started shaving, he had thought the mole was a hassle. When Simone began kissing it, he suddenly realized it was actually an asset.

Simone twirled around again and raised herself up on her toes like a ballet dancer. She gently planted a kiss on the mole on Andy's face—her lips like soft blossoms on his skin. His whole body came alive. Smiling, she put the cigarette back to his lips.

"Thank you," Andy mumbled with the cigarette pursed between his lips. He inhaled deeply and gazed at his beautiful girlfriend. Suddenly, he felt dizzy. He wondered if he had taken too long of a drag. No, it wasn't the drag. Andy's world felt like it shifted in some subtle and indefinable way. He was still himself, but he suddenly became aware of many things all at once—the way one does in a dream when reality suddenly crystallizes around a single moment.

Simone was no longer there. He felt like he understood that he had not seen her in many years. A miasma of smells assaulted him—stale sweat, antiseptic, and some kind of air freshener, the kind that just makes the air thicker instead of freshening it. He was so very tired, consumed with a bone-deep lethargy that turned his limbs to rubber, and his neck and shoulders ached from lying in one position too long. He didn't feel clean.

He was lying on his back. He had been lying down for a very long time; he couldn't remember when he'd last gotten out of bed. He couldn't turn his head. His neck was stiff, and the front of his throat felt strange—large and cumbersome—as if it no longer belonged to him. The back of his throat was sandpaper, and when he tried to swallow it felt as if shards of glass erupted from his flesh. Pain suffused his whole upper body, and he knew the intense feeling had come to stay. No amount of drugs or sleep would ever get rid of it. He began to panic.

Immediately, he lifted a shaky hand to his throat and felt the hard plastic tube taped in place. It vibrated as a machine hissed next to his bed. He was on a respirator. Fluids from a plastic bag dripped into a tube in his arm. More plastic tubes were in various other places. Cancer. Parts of his body had been removed; other parts were rotting from insidious disease. His stomach felt queasy from the drugs...

"Andy!" Simone's voice penetrated the fog. His world shifted in an instant, once again, and he looked down at her pretty face. She looked frightened, her sweet brown eyes full of worry. "Andy? What's wrong? Are you feeling okay?"

Had he been dreaming? It wasn't like any dream he had ever experienced; it had been so very *real*. He had been himself, only in a different time and place. Andy glanced down at the cigarette in his fingers, and then stared at it as if he held a live cobra. He tossed it to the ground, crushing it underneath the heel of his shoe.

"What are you doing?" Simone demanded. "You just lit that up! I didn't even get any." She made a cute little pouty face that Andy couldn't resist. His heart pounded, partly because of her and partly because of his strange vision.

"Ah, c'mon," he grinned. "We don't need no stinkin' ciggie! Damn things are cancer sticks. *Here's* what I need…" He swung Simone up by the waist, wrapping his strong arms around her and kissing her rose petal lips. Her slender arms slid up around his neck, feeling the smooth leather of the jacket. This was the Andy she knew and loved. She kissed him back and sighed happily. But in the back of her mind she wondered what had just happened. For a brief moment, Andy had seemed like someone else—someone she didn't know. He had almost looked as if he were *dying*. She mentally shook herself free of the ugly image and continued to kiss her boyfriend. Time dissolved for both of them.

§§§§§§

"Sorry we're late!" Simone said breathlessly from the front seat as Karen got into the car. Karen had been waiting in front of the convenience store for exactly thirty-three minutes. She knew this because she hadn't been able to stop staring at her watch as she waited for Andy and Simone to pick her up. The minutes had dragged on like hours.

"Got your stuff?" Simone asked, hoping Karen wasn't too annoyed. She flashed a smile. Lucky for her, Karen smiled back and patted the gym bag full of clothes on her lap. She nodded and decided to let the whole thing go.

It was impossible to be annoyed with Simone for long; it would've been like getting mad at a cute puppy. With her dream so close she could practically touch it, she had *wanted* to scream with frustration at Andy and Simone for making her wait—for deliberately keeping her from her destiny. But what was the point? What would it accomplish? Tonight was Tess Tramontine's night, and Karen wasn't going to let anyone or anything mess that up.

Not only was Tess the confident beauty that Karen was not, Tess also had a condom in her gym bag. She was set on losing her virginity to David tonight. No one knew this though, not even David himself. But he would find out soon enough. He wouldn't be able to resist her. Theirs would be a meeting of mind, body, and spirit—a joining of soulmates who had been waiting for each other all their lives. Yes, it was finally going to happen *now that Andy and Simone had finally brought the freaking transportation so she could finally get to her destiny at this freaking party! They had damn well better have brought the freaking red jacket that is going to make it all happen...*

"So, um, did you bring the jacket?" Karen asked Simone, with a tight smile. *Relax,* Karen told herself. *Tess is calm and self-assured. Tess is not uptight about anything. Nobody likes uptight. David won't like uptight. Uptight is not going to work.* She breathed deeply and felt a flutter in the pit of her stomach.

Simone beamed as she held up the jacket which had been on her lap. She passed it back to Karen. The scent of old leather and brass merry-go-round rings and the earth after a spring rain filled Karen's nose; she stroked the blood-colored folds. Tess was going to look stunning in this. *Radiant. Stunning. Sensuous.*

Andy and Simone chatted in the front seat as they drove to Melina's, and Karen did her best to be a part of the conversation. But so many images filled her mind that it was hard to concentrate. *How and when should she present the condom? Would it seem too forward? How would it fit into the beauty of their souls meeting for the first time? Should she ask him to get her a drink? Perhaps that would be a good idea. That's how it's done in the movies.*

"What?" Karen realized that Simone had said something to her.

"You're a million miles away!" Simone laughed. "We're parking in the back and then going in the kitchen door at Melina's. We can change in the bathroom. Ready, Freddy?" They had arrived. No, Tess had arrived.

§ § § § § §

"Karen, don't comb your hair down like that. You *know* it won't stay put," Simone admonished her. They were in a small bathroom off the kitchen of Melina's house. Simone stood on a little wooden stool behind Karen with a hairbrush in one hand and a can of hairspray in the other. Laughter and the clinking of bottles could already be heard outside the bathroom door.

Simone smiled at Karen's reflection in the mirror. *Karen, if you would stop fussing and worrying for two minutes, everyone would be able to see how pretty you already are,* she thought. Karen was one of the few girls who would still talk to Simone—now that she was dating Andy. The competition was ferocious. Karen was also one of the few girls who didn't have a crush on the star football player, probably figuring him to be out of her league. Well, David was out of her league, too, but Simone liked Karen too much to hurt her feelings by saying it. She would do whatever she could to help make this big night a success.

"It never stays put. It's always a mess," Karen lamented. Her reddish-brown hair couldn't decide whether to be curly or straight, so it compromised by frizzing instead. At the moment, she was horrified at how the hair on the right side of her head looked squashed down; the left side poofed out uncontrollably.

"I look like an accident victim," she moaned to Simone. "You know, where your head gets squashed and you're in a coma for six months, and no one thinks you'll ever come out of it but then one day you do and it's in all the papers?"

"Karen!" Simone scolded. She sighed and grabbed the comb from her. "Puh-lease! Stop being so dramatic!" She ran her hand through Karen's hair. "Let your hair be free. Let it do what nature wants it to do—here, like this," She ran her hands under the running tap water and then gently wetted Karen's hair a little. Then she ran her fingers through it again. "See? Just let it wave and curl however it wants to. It's pretty like this!"

Karen scrutinized her appearance in the mirror. *Mom would call this messy hair. But it's really windblown and free. And if I put anymore makeup over these zits, I'm gonna look like Amy Winehouse.*

"Here, put a little more blush on; it highlights your cheekbones," Simone said, already brushing color onto Karen's cheeks. It was clear that Karen was unaccustomed to wearing makeup and things were a little lopsided.

The red stiletto shoes didn't fit very well; they pinched Karen's toes. She didn't want any panty-lines marring the black skirt, but thong underwear was a little weird. She hoped the zipper wouldn't break as she sucked in her gut and struggled to pull the skirt up. The spaghetti-strap top didn't come down far enough, and she couldn't decide whether to try tucking it in or not. Finally, she left it out. *Karen is fat, but Tess is voluptuous,* she reminded herself, trying to find a little confidence.

Simone had done all she could do. "See you out there!" she said with a smile. She quickly smoothed out her electric blue nylon dress in front of the mirror, blew Karen a kiss, and slipped out the bathroom door. Karen stared after her, her mouth going dry. She was on her own now. She took a deep breath and put on the red jacket. *This works,* she thought with a nod. She ran her fingers through her hair one last time, took another deep breath, and took a final look in the mirror herself.

Tess looked back at her. Her wavy reddish-brown hair fell gracefully over the collar of the red jacket; the glittery earrings sparkled in the light. The black tank top showed voluptuous curves under the open leather jacket, playfully exposing a hint of midriff. Long legs emerged from the tight black skirt. The glossy red heels provided sass and style. The clunky glasses were long gone, and the image in the mirror was a little out-of-focus—Lynne's contact lenses weren't exactly the right prescription for Karen—but it was obvious that Tess was beautiful. For the first time in her life, Karen felt *beautiful.*

"Hi, my name is Tess," she said to the image in the mirror, tossing her hair. "I'm Tess. What's up?" She turned her head turned to the side and smiled coyly at the mirror. "Dude, I'm Tess..." Finally, she turned to leave the bathroom. *I'm ready,* she thought.

But her hand froze for a moment on the door handle. She could hear the party revving up on the other side of the door. *How easily Simone had slipped right through this door, as if she belongs out there, as if she's done it a hundred times.* Karen's heart raced; her stomach tightened. *It's just a door. All I have to do is turn the handle and open it...*

She took one more deep breath and flung the door open. It was time to find David.

§ § § § §

It was close to midnight. By then, Karen had already consumed two beers, three cups of spiked punch, four Ding Dongs, a handful of chips and salsa, a chocolate chip cookie, and an unidentified little pink thing with icing on it. Her feet were killing her, and David was nowhere to be found.

The music was thunderous, and the living room was packed with dancing, sweating bodies. It didn't take long for Karen to become too hot in the leather jacket, but she refused to take it off. Her hair kept getting tangled in the long earrings, and Simone had put so much makeup on her that her mascara was starting to run. Her stomach rumbled; the mixture of sugar, salsa, chips, and alcohol was not a happy combination. This was only the third time she had ever drunk alcohol, and she was decidedly feeling buzzed.

Maybe David wasn't coming? What had happened to him? What if he had had some terrible accident on the way to the party? Karen's imagination reeled off into several directions at once, with sirens flashing and paramedics scraping him off the freeway. *If he'd been badly injured, she, Tess, would be there to comfort him. She would stay with him in the hospital around the clock, dabbing his forehead and holding his hand. She would get to know his family, and they would be grateful for her help and her obvious love for their son, and—*

"Karen? Is that you?" a voice called out, interrupting her thoughts.

Karen whirled around, a little too quickly, and three things happened all at once. Moments before, she had taken one shoe off in order to rub her aching toes along the back of her leg. The sudden distraction startled her, making her lose her balance, and so she nearly fell down. At the same time, she blinked hard as she turned around, causing the contact lens in her right eye to pop out. It was immediately lost forever in the netherworld of party detritus at her feet. Now she couldn't see properly unless she closed her right eye and just looked out of her left. Furthermore, as she opened her mouth to say, "Hey, David! What a pleasant surprise!" the chemistry experiment taking place in her stomach released a large volume of vaporized gases that had been under high pressure. The resulting vibrations as they rushed through her upper airways created a deafening explosion.

Instead of seeing Tess Tramontine's party debut, David was treated to a lurching, swaying Karen Little on one foot, with streaky eye makeup, one eye squeezed closed, and a thunderous belch blasting forth. She would have made a horde of Vikings proud.

"Hi, uh…Karen," David said uncertainly.

Color flooded into Karen's face. *This is not happening. What exactly is happening? This must be a nightmare,* Karen thought. Her heart started to pound. Frantically, she tried to organize her body parts in a more suitable arrangement—opening her right eye, closing her mouth (too late), stabilizing her legs and feet—but the alcohol had made her woozy and uncoordinated. She overshot her efforts and ended up blinking and opening her eyes too wide, swaying too far the other way, and opening and closing her mouth several times like a fish out of water.

David wondered if she were about to have some kind of seizure. He glanced anxiously at the girl standing next to him, and then back at Karen. "Karen, this is uh, my girlfriend, Amanda," he stammered. David's girlfriend smiled, but she looked like she was trying hard not to laugh.

Karen stared dumbly at her crush and then at the cute dark-haired girl with him. *Girlfriend? He has a girlfriend? He's not supposed to have a girlfriend!* Her pulse formed a hurricane in her ears. She barely heard Amanda's polite greeting. Instead, she simply muttered, "Nice to meet you…" and staggered out of the room on one shoe. She left what was left of her dignity next to the contact lens on the floor.

Outside on the back porch in the cool backyard, the tears came. Karen huddled in a lawn chair, bent over with her arms around her knees. Sobs shook her shoulders. She was stunned that so much pain, humiliation, and embarrassment could exist with such ferocity inside of her. An endless loop replayed in her mind with savage intensity: belching into her beloved David's face, his look of shock and confusion, and those awful, fateful words: *Bellllch! Karen, this is my girlfriend, Amanda. Bellllch! Karen, this is my girlfriend, Amanda. Bellllch! Karen, this is my girlfriend, Amanda…*

She would not be able to return to school. There was no telling how many people at the party had witnessed her supreme humiliation, and in fact, they were almost certainly all laughing at her now. If they weren't now, they would be.

A hand fell softly on her shoulder, a gentle caress. Karen lifted up her swollen, tear-streaked face.

"Here, drink this," a man's voice murmured in her ear. A red plastic cup of water appeared at her lips. It tasted sweet, cool, and refreshing. The gentle voice derailed the horrible endless loop in her head.

He was kneeling in front of her, wiping her face with a napkin. She couldn't see very well, missing a contact lens, but the man was smiling kindly. He was perhaps in his late twenties, with curly brown hair and hazel eyes, like hers. Or were they greenish-brown? She wasn't quite sure.

"Is greenish-brown the same thing as hazel?" Karen asked him while trying to compose herself.

His eyes danced for a second. He grinned. "If you say so," he replied. "I'm Glen. I'm a friend of Melina's brother, Dan. What's your name, you little wet kitten?"

Karen stared at him. It seemed to her she was looking into a mirror. His eyes were so much like her own. She smiled back. He seemed warm and inviting. Even better, he wasn't laughing at her. "Tess," she finally whispered.

"Tess? Well, why don't we find a better place to sit?" Glen suggested. He glanced up at the bug light above them. It wasn't a great atmosphere, and several loud guys burst out of the kitchen door onto the patio. They were drunk, laughing and throwing things at each other.

Glen took Karen's hands and pulled her to her feet. "Come on," he said in her ear. "I know a place we can go."

The sleeve of the red jacket brushed Glen's wrist as she started tottering after him. His fingers slowly entwined in hers. An odd feeling filled her for a moment, and she shivered, stopping for a moment to catch her breath.

Things were different. Karen wasn't here and now; she was someplace else. Glen was still with her. What a look he had on his face as she told him something—some kind of important news. His face was full of scorn, and he jeered at her. She suddenly felt like the biggest fool in the world. "Stop your blubbering," he was saying to her. She was humiliated all over again, and terrified—but of what? It was undoubtedly something awful…something huge and forbidding…something she couldn't quite understand in her foggy, drunken state, but she knew she was missing something important—something that could change everything.

Karen pulled back, unlocking her fingers out of Glen's. Fear clutched at her heart, and she had the urge to turn and go—to leave Glen and the party behind her and go home. *If I stop now, it will all be okay.* Where had this thought come from? She felt very warm inside the red jacket, as if it was enveloping her in an embrace, but she knew that something wasn't right. *It's time for me to go home—before it's too late.*

"What's the matter?" Glen asked her, his eyes full of concern. His hands were soft and sure, caressing her shoulders, pulling her close. "There's nothing to be afraid of," he murmured. His voice was like honey and silk mixed together. "I'll look after you." He looked at her with such intensity, such desire, that she realized he was looking at Tess—not Karen. Tess took a deep breath, took his hand again, and followed his lead.

Still sniffling, Karen got into a car when he opened the door for her. Glen's arm was wrapped solicitously around her shoulders, and he tenderly helped her as she swayed getting into the car.

"Where are we going?" she asked when he was seated in the driver's seat. He really had the most beautiful brown eyes—green eyes—what color *were* they? The engine started but Karen didn't notice when the car started to move away from the curb. She let her head rest back against the headrest for just a moment. She was so very tired, and the tears kept slipping out from underneath her closed eyelids, ruining her makeup even more.

Glen didn't answer. Instead, he kept driving.

"I don't know why, I can't stop—crying," Karen mumbled. "I'm always like that. Once I start, I can't seem to..." Another great belch rumbled forth, but Karen was dozing off and didn't seem to notice.

She didn't notice when the car stopped either—or when her door opened. Somebody was helping her out of the car. What was his name again? Gary? Glen? Greg? "I have to get my...glasses..." she said to him. He murmured something back to her, but she wasn't sure what it was. Nor did she really care.

And then they were in a bedroom. Karen could no longer tell whether what was happening was really happening, or if it was all some kind of dream inside of her alcoholic stupor. *This must be a dream. If this is real, then Tess Tramon—Tromin—Trampoline looks like she's half-naked on a bed. Something happened to her black skirt. And this guy—his name is Glen—is doing something with her. He's on top of her...*

......Tess, are you doing this? If you don't want to do this, now would be a really, really good time to stop. I think this is actually really happening. This isn't David. This isn't Jax. Do you know where your condom is? Is this guy even wearing one?

"No...No..." Karen whispered, but the dream was so strong she couldn't tell if she'd said it out loud or not. She did know that Glen was on top of her. And that she felt pain and discomfort. *No. This must be a dream. This is not how I was going to lose my virginity. Becoming a woman is supposed to be beautiful and fulfilling and life-changing. Not...this. Not this. Not this. Not this. Not this.*

This felt like what had happened with Jerry, her stepfather—how he had tried forcing himself on her, and she kept resisting him. She had been filled with confusion, fear, and despair, feeling shameful and tainted. Finally, she told her mother. But what followed after that became the worst time of her life—recriminations, legal action, divorce...a family torn apart.

Suddenly, a fiercely suppressed dream blazed to the surface: the hopeless vision of losing her virginity to Jax, the one she had always loved. She imagined Jax—the most beautiful, most intelligent, most amazing person—touching her with the sweetest of caresses; she'd hoped they'd someday be together forever. David Steinberg was simply a replacement, albeit the most beautiful one she could find, but when her heart of hearts was laid bare it was Jax who dwelt there.

The vision made her cry even more. She had spent the last two years trying to suppress and lose the intense feelings she had for her best friend, knowing in her heart that Jax would never know—he would never understand. He didn't look at her that way; he had never thought of her as anyone besides Boogerhead. But in her dream, Jax would be caring and sweet, and he would already know how she felt about him. His gorgeous eyes would be filled with sensuous desire and love for her only; his touch would be magic. The precious moments they would share would never be like this—this awful spectacle of grunting and sweating with someone she didn't even know.

Glen finished and got off the bed. Karen's tears returned and she sobbed as if her heart were breaking. Glen turned and looked at her in disgust. "Oh, stop your blubbering," he said, pulling on his pants.

She stared at him, shocked. For a single lucid moment, she wondered how she had ever thought he was a nice guy, or that his eyes were anything other than dull dishwater gray. *This was it. This was the big moment, and it was with a guy I don't even know. Date-rape. No, I am not dumb enough to get raped. It was just—I was just—I can't believe I will never have a first time again. I was wasted during my first time. And it was with a guy who just used me. I am such a loser.*

"Take—take—me home—right now," she sobbed, and he did.

DAY FOUR

The red jacket actually fit Jax perfectly. It was a little tight on Andy, and way too big for Celeste and Simone, but it seemed like it had been made especially for Jax. The dark red leather complemented his light coffee-colored skin, warm brown eyes, and curly, glossy dark brown hair that was cut short on the sides and a little longer on the top. His hair and coloring were legacies of his white mother and black father—birth parents he had never known. As far as he was concerned, Zack and Charlotte Montclair were his real parents; they were a loving white couple who had adopted him when he was three months old. The Montclairs never had any biological children of their own, but two younger adopted brothers had joined the family after Jax.

Someday, maybe he would step into the realm of finding his birth parents, but not now. That whole thing was too big, too huge—a giant labyrinth with so many trapdoors that he wouldn't even know where to begin. *Someday.*

Now Jax's heart was filled with music: music that he heard in his head; music that he scribbled on notepads; and music that he played on his guitar. Mattresses, heavy blankets, and Spider-Man sheets were nailed to the walls of his bedroom—a makeshift soundproof studio to practice in whenever he pleased. Spider-Man had always been his favorite superhero because of his ability to expand outward in all directions. He could easily explore his whole environment, never letting mere physical obstacles get in his way. Spiderman reinvented himself every time he put on his Spidey suit.

Music did this for Jax. If he couldn't actually climb a skyscraper with his hands and feet, his music could take his mind and spirit anywhere and everywhere. He had composed fifty-seven songs, most of which were carefully written out on staff paper in a special notebook. Eleven years of piano lessons had made him an excellent musician, and he was often called upon to play at school functions. But singing and playing guitar were his true passions. This audition was his first real opportunity to show what he could do in an actual professional setting, and he had a folder full of photocopies of his best original pieces to show the band, Seventh Heaven.

Jax had taken the bus downtown and was walking to a converted warehouse, looking for an address he had scribbled on a scrap of paper. He glanced in a store window as he passed by, checking out his reflection to see what the band leader would see. He hoped he didn't look like some geeky high school kid; the red jacket was supposed to take care of that.

The reflection of the boy who stared back at him was of medium height and medium build. His curly dark brown hair looked decent; his shadow of a mustache and a few straggling whiskers on both sides of his chin made him appear artsy. Jax hoped to grow to six feet, but he seemed to have leveled out at approximately five feet, nine inches. He was slender, but worked out with weights to try and bulk up a little. (However, weightlifting had resulted in minimal success so far.) He nodded at himself in the store window as he admired the outfit he had carefully put together: shades, t-shirt, jeans, Nikes—and of course, the red leather jacket.

Karen had been right about the vintage jacket. It *was* pretty cool, and it looked good on him. *Like the Spidey suit. Maybe I'll keep it in a secret chamber, and whenever I want I'll duck into a secret doorway, put on the red jacket, slide down the secret chute into my waiting Maserati, and take off, arriving at the recording studio as Jax of Azteca, the new and ultra cool band...*

Knowing he was being neurotic, Jax set his guitar case down on the sidewalk and slung his backpack off his shoulder to look inside of it one more time. The music folder with the photocopies was there; he hadn't forgotten it. He had agonized for a week over which of his songs to bring, and had finally settled on nine of his best, including his very favorite, "Lightning Sky." It would just be too geeky to show up with a huge thick folder of *all* of his music—like he was trying too hard. He figured it would be much better to stun the band first with an offhand showing of a few choice songs, amaze them with his genius, and then remark casually that he had more at home. *I'd be happy to bring some to the next rehearsal...*

For these nine songs, he had written out the charts for lead guitar, bass guitar, rhythm guitar, vocals, keyboard, and drums. He even had a flute part for the synthesizer if the band had one. But it could be done without it. *Okay, I need to stop psyching myself out. I'll be fine,* he told himself, taking a few deep breaths to calm his nerves.

He picked up his guitar and kept walking, his pace quickening along with his heartbeat. They were sure to love "Lightning Sky." This was going to be the cover title for the album he would someday produce with his own band, Azteca. His band would have a manager, and a bus, and it would perform all over the country, all while selling millions of albums.

Jax's imagination ran away with him. He saw himself as the new leader of Seventh Heaven, after Luke, the current leader, had some unfortunate but non-life-threatening problem and had to step down. The rest of the band would unanimously vote him in as leader, despite his youth, because of his obvious talent and how he had an uncanny ability to bring them all together and make music the likes of which no one had ever experienced before. They would later explain all of this during televised interviews with newscasters, before and after live concerts. *As much as we miss Luke, the original leader of the band, he just didn't have Jax's creative genius. He's really revolutionized our whole sound, and we're privileged to be working with him...*

With its ho-hum name changed to the edgier, sleeker Azteca, the band soon would rise all the way to the top. Jax would probably have to study for the high school equivalency exam since he would be so busy touring, writing music, rehearsing with the group, and making appearances on TV. He wouldn't have time to go to high school anymore.

He would miss his friends, but this was his career calling. This was it; from now on he wasn't going to be some obscure kid with a guitar. He was about to become Jax, leader of Azteca, and he was psyched. He considered just going by Jax and dropping his last name, hoping his adoptive parents wouldn't be offended. *Jax, on its own, had a ring to it. He was a child of the world—a child between cultures, an orphan with parents—and 'Jax' would embrace all of this in its elegant simplicity. He wasn't excluding anyone, just speaking to a larger calling.*

He glanced at the address on the slip of paper in his hand again. The guy on the phone had said to go around the back of the warehouse and up a staircase. He had found the staircase just fine. Now he was in front of a door. He took a deep breath and knocked.

Nothing happened. He knocked again, and waited, shifting from foot to foot. Was this the right place? It didn't look like much was happening here. There were no numbers on the door at the top of the staircase, but he was pretty sure this was the right place. He knocked again, and a fluttery feeling erupted in the pit of his stomach. What if he were lost? What if they were all ready and waiting for him somewhere else, and he had blown it, showing up at some other location? If he had to call the band for help finding the place, he would look like the biggest moron. *First impressions are everything,* he told himself, getting more anxious as he stood there. *I'm so much younger than them. I can't afford to come across as some dumb kid. If that happens, it will be impossible to wow them with my music—*

The door creaked open. Marijuana smoke greeted Jax first. It was followed by a face that peered out from the dark interior.

"Yeah?" a guy in his mid-twenties asked. He was white, and skinny, with shaggy brown hair and pocked cheeks from what Jax could see.

"Hi, I'm Jax—Jaxon Montclair?" Jax stammered, *Oops, I meant to just stick with Jax.*

Silence. "Yeah?" the guy repeated, as if Jax hadn't said anything.

"Um, I'm here for the audition? Nine o'clock, Saturday, the fourteenth?" Jax waited. This guy didn't seem to know what he was talking about. The shaggy-haired guy grunted and closed the door on Jax's face.

Dumbfounded, Jax wasn't sure what to do next. *What did that mean? Was it caveman for 'Please, make yourself comfortable on the cement steps while I fetch my master?' or was it more along the lines of 'Get lost! We don't know nothin' 'bout no audition!'? Did it simply mean 'Dude, you're at the wrong place'?*

Jax began to turn his back when suddenly the door creaked open again. The shaggy-haired guy had returned with another guy in his mid- to late-twenties—a black man with a shaved head and a soul patch. He had small diamond studs in both ears. *Is this Luke? Am I standing in front of the Seventh Heaven band?*

The guy looked Jax up and down, taking in the guitar case and the backpack.

Jax decided to try and start over. He smiled. "I'm Jax. I'm here for the audition?" *Damn. I should've said something cooler. I sound like an idiot.*

The guy's eyes stayed fixated on Jax, but he stepped back and motioned with his head into the dark interior, inviting Jax in. He followed, carrying his guitar case, and the shaggy-haired guy closed the door behind them.

A dark corridor opened up into a loft, with old carpets strewn on the floor and sagging couches against two walls. A small makeshift stage had been built at the far end of the loft, with three rickety wooden steps leading up to it. A tangle of cables and wires crept all over as if a mutant electronic jungle were taking over. Two keyboards, several guitar stands, a drum set, and a whole collection of speakers and amps were jammed onto the small stage. The musicians themselves were strewn about on the couches and carpets, smoking and drinking casually. A thick layer of cigarette and pot smoke hung in the air, making Jax's eyes water.

He realized he had been holding his breath ever since crossing the threshold and let it out in a big sigh. At least he was in the right place.

He stopped in the middle of the floor with half a dozen people looking at him—some with mild interest, some with none. One guy lay on his back on the floor with his eyes closed. Pizza boxes and beer cans littered the floor around him.

"Hey, guys," Jax said uncertainly, realizing as he said it that there were two women among them. *Whoops,* he thought.

The man with the soul patch looked at him. "What'd you say your name was, dude?"

"Jax, I'm Jax," Jax replied eagerly.

The man nodded. "How old are you?"

"Eighteen, I'm eighteen." *Relax! You don't have to repeat every single thing.* Jax's heart picked up the pace a little; he was unaccustomed to telling lies, but he just couldn't bring himself to say that he was only sixteen years old. They all looked so much older than him. The man asking all of the questions, who did turn out to be Luke, grunted and smirked. Clearly, he had his doubts about Jax's age.

"I brought my guitar," Jax offered, and immediately wished he could take it back. *As if there could be any doubt about what's inside my guitar case, for crying out loud.* "And some charts I wrote…" he added lamely.

"Uh huh," said Luke. "We're on a break right now. You can jam a little with us in a few minutes, and we'll see what you've got." He disappeared down another dark hallway, leaving Jax stranded in the middle of the mismatched carpets and pizza boxes.

He put his guitar case down and sat on the end of the couch nearest him, a moth-eaten creation that had definitely seen better days—like during the Depression. He glanced at the woman sitting next to him and offered his hand.

"I'm Jax," he said—*and now everyone has heard my name three times; does that seem like enough?*—and smiled at her, trying not to look as nervous as he felt.

She took his hand and smiled back at him. "Jasmine," she replied. "How ya doing?" Jax noticed that she was actually quite pretty. She was black, with long braids, and soft brown eyes that were accented with greenish eye makeup. She seemed very laidback and sophisticated, and Jax couldn't help noticing her low-cut spandex shirt and the swell of her breasts. Suddenly, the designation of pretty was elevated to beautiful.

He wanted to say something more to her but decided instead to busy himself with his guitar. He took it out of its case and wiped it down with a chamois—as if he hadn't done this a dozen times already today. Next, he worked intently on tuning the strings, using a tuning fork produced from a little drawstring bag his mom had made for him.

A warm hand rested on his forearm and he turned to look at Jasmine.

"We have the guitars all wired up," she told him, with a smile. "We're not using acoustic guitars."

"Oh. Yeah. Sure," Jax answered quickly, looking down at his guitar. *Of course they're using electric guitars.* That was fine. That was cool. Hadn't he told his dad a hundred times that he needed an electric guitar as well as an acoustic one? But his dad had pointed out that then he would want all the equipment that goes along with an electric guitar—the amps, cords, and cables—and they weren't quite ready to have that much noise in the house. They also didn't want to spend that much money. Jax didn't have the extra cash either.

He put the guitar away and waited, wondering when would be a good time to offer his own charts. Should he start with "Lightning Sky," his best work? Or should he lead up to it, maybe starting with "Obsession" and "Random Destination," and then bring out "Lightning Sky"?

Someone suddenly passed Jax a joint, and he tried to keep calm. He had never smoked marijuana before. He nodded, took it a bit awkwardly, and inhaled. He hadn't expected it to be so harsh, but the abrasive smoke charred his throat all the way down, making him gag and cough. He was still coughing when Luke came back from wherever he had gone. He headed up the three steps to the stage, and the rest of the band members straggled up to join him.

Apparently, Jasmine played keyboards for the band. Luke was lead singer and played lead guitar. The shaggy-haired guy, whose name was Curt, played bass guitar. The drummer was another skinny white guy—the one who had been lying on the floor; Jax thought his name was Drake, but he wasn't sure. Luke instructed Jax to play rhythm guitar and sing backup vocals with Jasmine and Curt.

The music was fast—much faster than Jax was expecting. It was hard to keep up, reading the chord changes for the guitar and trying to sing the scribbled, nearly illegible words. To make matters worse, he *still* kept coughing from the pot smoke he had inhaled. His voice felt and sounded rough, and he wasn't used to singing into a microphone. At first he was too close to the mike, causing it to make popping and crackling noises, until Luke told him move back a little bit. (Jax hadn't known it was him causing the sounds.) But then Jax ending up moving too far away from the microphone, and Luke had to reposition him again.

Jax sang and played three songs with the band and hoped everyone liked what they heard. After his brief set, he was relegated to the couch again. He listened to the band play for another two hours, and even began to somewhat relax. Unfortunately for him, he never had a chance to show the band his own music. He knew his voice hadn't sounded very good; his throat was irritated and kept seizing up; and he had made some mistakes on the chord changes on the guitar. (However, he knew he had gotten better by the third song.) He wasn't given another chance to get back up there and play again, and he was too chicken to bring it up. He was dying to get his own guitar out and play his music for them—*then* the band would see what he was made of. But how could he make this happen without coming across as foolish? Soon, Luke seemed to forget Jax was there altogether.

Seventh Heaven finished playing around midnight. Or at least it *looked* like the band was finished. Was the group just taking another break? Would Jax be able to perform his own music now?

It didn't seem likely. Luke held out his hand and grinned. "Thanks a lot for stopping by, man," he said with a nod. Jax shook the man's hand. His heart sunk. Apparently, his audition was over. He knew he hadn't done very well, and the last buses ran at 11:30 P.M.

Five minutes later, he was back out on the cement staircase behind the warehouse, carrying his guitar and his backpack; they both suddenly felt much heavier than they had on his way to the audition. He wondered if his mom would kill him if he called her and asked her to come and pick him up. She usually went to bed around 10:00 P.M.

Perhaps he should call Karen instead? Could she get her mom's car? He'd thought he'd be finished before the last bus left the station—and in fact he *had* been finished before then, but he had sat around waiting. For what? He didn't know. Either way, now it was too late. He didn't have enough money for a taxi. Frustrated and tired, he tried to figure out how many miles it was back to his house. Five? Seven? More?

A voice stopped him and he turned around. It was Jasmine. He'd been hoping to get away quickly and quietly in an attempt to minimize his humiliation. No such luck.

"Hold up, my man," she said, coming down the stairs. She was wearing a shiny black coat, and her spike-heeled boots made her cautious on the steps. "You got wheels?" she asked him.

"No," he answered. "I'm taking the bus."

She caught up to him and smiled sympathetically. "Buses are done for the night, you know. Unless you live around the corner, you're gonna be walking a *long* time."

Jax just stood looking at her, waiting for some smooth repartee to flow from his mouth, but none came. She was right, he *did* have a long walk ahead of him, and it would have been a lot cooler if he had his own car, but he didn't. He was still just a sixteen-year-old kid who'd missed the bus—sadly, in more ways than one.

Jasmine shifted her shoulder bag and tilted her head at him. "Come on, I'll give you a lift." She started walking ahead of him toward her vehicle. Jax was so surprised it didn't occur to him that she hadn't asked him where he lived.

"Oh, um, thanks," Jax mumbled appreciatively. He hurried after her sweetly swaying tight jeans. In a matter of seconds, his whole evening had changed in a direction he could hardly fathom. He breathed deeply, trying to quell the fluttering in his stomach. *Relax. Spider-Man is always cool, no matter what comes up. And chicks dig him.*

Once they were both in Jasmine's car, Jax struggled with the seatbelt for an embarrassingly long time. They drove in silence for a few minutes before he managed to get it together enough to ask Jasmine about the band, about how she'd gotten involved, and where she thought it was going. She explained that Luke had invited her to join the band two years ago; she had participated in a few professional gigs. Currently, Seventh Heaven was working on an album.

"Is Luke your boyfriend?" Jax blurted out. *Ohmigod. Where did that just come from?*

Jasmine glanced at him in the darkened interior of the car. She raised her right eyebrow and hesitated for a second. "He was," she finally said. "We broke up."

A large silence filled the space between them, and Jax's recklessness suddenly ran out.

"So, didn't you have some music you brought?" Jasmine asked, changing the subject. "Your own stuff?"

"Yes!" he answered, relieved. She seemed interested, so he started telling her about his music: how he'd gotten started writing two years ago; how he was experimenting with adding woodwinds and strings to a fusion base; and even where he got his ideas for lyrics. She seemed receptive and easy to talk to. *Maybe I do still have a chance.*

"I have two friends who play violin; sometimes we jam together," Jax began to explain. "One of them is this crazy-talented chick who wins state competitions all the time." He suddenly didn't think he should be talking about Celeste at this moment. Somehow, a taboo on bringing up other women had materialized. He didn't want to give the slightest impression to Jasmine that he could be interested in someone else.

Jasmine parked the car in front of an apartment building but didn't get out. They continued talking for an hour though—Jasmine listening intently and asking the right questions as Jax poured himself out. His face remained excited, alive, and animated throughout the entire conversation. During the audition, he had been closed and guarded. Now he felt that he was with someone who really understood him. He rarely opened up to anyone like this about his music, simply because there were hardly any other people who had the interest or the right ears to understand where he was coming from. Jasmine seemed to have both. She knew instantly what he was talking about as he tried to express his ideas.

To Jax's amazement, he discovered himself revealing dreams and ideas to her that he had never spoken aloud. At the same time, he found himself getting more and more lost in her doe-brown eyes as she listened to him. She was so very feminine, yet not dumb; she had savvy and street-smarts that she wore as naturally as he wore the red jacket. He couldn't help wondering what those beautiful breasts would look like released from their spandex confinement...

"Jax," she said, bringing him back to reality. Her voice was low and relaxed, and her hand on Jax's thigh. "Sing your best original song for me—right here, right now."

He gulped quietly. No one had ever heard "Lightning Sky" before. It was an embryo developed inside his own imagination, with his charts and guitar and keyboard inside his cloistered mattress-padded bedroom at home.

Jax realized that Jasmine was genuinely interested in his song. She wasn't just indulging a little whim or playing with him. She had asked him as an adult—woman to man—to hear his song. He felt inspired. About a hundred other dizzying emotions Jax had never experienced entered his heart and mind all at once.

His voice had recovered from the smoky assault, and he filled the car with a quiet, silky baritone—his voice was warm and full of feeling without being overly sentimental. Jasmine held his hand as he sang. He could tell that she was getting it. She understood the song and its sweet blend of hope and longing…of the paradox of desire and uncertainty…of how life can turn a dream upside down and then change it into something full of magic. He finished and they sat in silence, simply letting thoughts and memories linger. He had never felt so comfortable with a woman before.

"Come inside," she said to him, still holding his hand. "I want to hear you sing it with the guitar."

Her apartment was small and dark, and he set the guitar case down so that he could take off the red jacket. As it hung open, Jasmine put her hands on his chest, leaning forward to inhale the coat's aroma.

"I love the smell of leather, don't you?" she asked, grinning. She gently kissed him on the cheek.

Time shifted and Jax felt as if he were standing inside a tunnel, or some kind of a narrow room without any ceiling. He was confused and filled with dread. He saw Jasmine and felt a little better. But she seemed different—out of it. She was lying on a sagging, derelict couch, like the one in the warehouse where the band held its practices, only this wasn't the same one. She didn't speak.

She was sick—very, very sick. She had lost a lot of weight, too, so that her cheeks were sunken in and her eyes were no longer alive. They were hollow, and the lids hung over them like dark rose petals—bruised ones from a wilted blossom. The braids were gone from her hair, which was frizzy, dull, and brown. Her once-clear skin was now blotchy. A cracked scab at the corner of her mouth looked painful, and she breathed as if her ribs were fragile eggshells. Those wonderful breasts had deflated with catastrophic weight loss, and her skin stretched tightly over her bones.

"Uh, Jax?" Jasmine had taken a step back from him, seeing a strange look on his face. "Is everything okay with you?"

Jax finished removing the red jacket and dropped it on the floor. The bizarre vision vanished, and he was back in her apartment. Jasmine appeared as living and vibrant and desirable as ever as she stood directly in front of him. A million questions were in her eyes.

"No problem," he smiled at her, and fought a lingering memory of her sunken eyes and flattened breasts. How could this beautiful, sexy woman who was so full of life carry death within her like that? It was impossible. It had just been some anomaly, some trick of the mind. Jax bent down to pick up the guitar case, but put it down again when he looked up to discover that Jasmine had already taken her shirt off.

The red jacket lay in a heap on the floor, forgotten.

DAY TWELVE

"So, what's this guy's name?" Connor asked Celeste as they put away their instruments. It was Tuesday afternoon and they had just finished rehearsing for an upcoming concert.

"Tranh," Celeste replied, rolling her eyes. "What else would it be? Just like half of the Vietnamese guys on the East Coast!" She snapped her violin case shut and slipped her music folder inside of her backpack. "And I can tell you what he'll be like even before I meet him: four-eyed, gawky, nerdy, belt cinched up to his armpits—I can't wait."

Connor laughed at the mental image. There was nothing gawky about him. He wore his tawny good looks naturally, without vanity, and greeted everyone equally, with an open, honest face. "Where did your parents find *this* guy? This isn't the guy whose family lives over the donut shop, right?" He knew Celeste was only allowed to date guys approved by her family, and they had never been comfortable with her friendship with him.

Celeste had a bright, sharp energy to her intelligent brown eyes. Where Connor was laidback, quiet, and sensitive, Celeste was observant, competitive, and ambitious. She moved through each day with drive and determination, being the best she could be. At the same time, she seemed to always be looking for something, trying to find some kind of path between her family heritage and the American world into which she had been born. Her past, present, and future were closely scrutinized by her family, leaving little room for Celeste herself.

She tossed her glossy raven-black hair and rolled her eyes at Connor. "Nope, thank God. My auntie's cousin's son owns a garage in Philadelphia, and one of his employees has a nephew who's in college. He's in town for two days for a family event, and they've hooked us up. Apparently, Tranh's ancestors come from the right side of the mountains in Vietnam."

Connor shook his head in wonder. "I don't even know who my ancestors were. Scottish, I think? Maybe some English?" He shrugged casually.

Celeste sighed as they walked down the hallway together, heading for the jacket's locker. "If I like this guy, I'm supposed to finish high school, go to the music conservatory, and then have a brief but brilliant career as a world-class violinist. I would marry this guy and produce grandchildren for our parents," she explained.

"All before you're thirty?" Connor asked in amazement.

"Uh huh," she chuckled. "It's pretty much all planned out." They stopped in front of the locker, and Celeste opened the padlock. They had all memorized the combination, and were supposed to return the red jacket to its locker so the next person could get it during his or her scheduled time. Celeste opened the locker door and removed the jacket. She smiled and stroked its soft red leather.

"But I'll tell you one thing," Celeste said as she turned to Connor, slipping the jacket on, her eyes bright and intense. "I intend to have a life—my *own* life. And it's not going to be with some geeky guy named Tranh."

Connor laughed again. She loved the way his eyes crinkled. She especially liked how his slightly crooked front tooth showed when he smiled. It gave his face an endearing quality. "Celeste, the supermodel," he teased.

"That's 'C' to you!" Celeste replied playfully. She turned up the sleeves of the red jacket and picked up her violin case. "Have you ever heard of 'middle C'?"

"I believe I have heard of it, yes," Connor answered, raising his eyebrows. It was pretty much the most basic note on the piano every schoolchild who took piano lessons learned.

"Well, I'm going to call myself Model C! I'll be on the covers of *Vogue* and *Cosmopolitan* and all of the big fashion magazines. I'm going to have penthouses in New York and Paris. I'll even have a Bichon Frise dog. It will travel with me wherever I go."

"Don't you need to be about three feet taller?" Connor wanted to know.

"Oh, what*ever*," Celeste sighed, swinging her purse at him and bopping him in the chest. "I was going to invite you to hang out with me in Paris and New York after I became rich and famous, but now I guess not!"

They passed through the double doors and left the school, walking out to the parking lot. "Have you talked to Karen yet? Didn't she go to Melina's party on Friday?" Connor wondered.

"Simone was there and she told me Karen looked great," Celeste said. "She wore the jacket and everything."

"That's cool! Sounds like she had a good time then," Connor nodded.

"Well, not exactly," Celeste continued. She hesitated a moment before going into detail. "You know how she has the hots for David Steinberg?"

Connor chuckled. "Everybody has the hots for David Steinberg—including his *girlfriend,*" he said sarcastically.

"Yeah, well, Karen missed the memo on the whole girlfriend thing," Celeste said, crinkling her nose. "Or maybe thought she would wow him anyway, but, um, not so much…"

"Oh, man. Poor girl," Connor said. He opened Celeste's car door for her and then walked around to his side before driving her home.

"Apparently, Karen had a little too much to drink and ended up sitting outside bawling her eyes out," Celeste went on. She buckled her seatbelt. "But then she got picked up by some friend of Melina's brother—some older guy…"

Connor buckled his own seatbelt and then stopped and stared at her. "*And?*" he prodded.

"And that's all I know!" Celeste shrugged. "You'll have to ask Karen for the juicy details."

"What! *That's all you know?* You girls and your gossip network—you know I depend on you for all the details! You can't just toss me a bone like that and leave me hanging! Did she get into his car? Was there tongue involved?" Connor asked.

"Connor!" Celeste screamed at him, giggling. It was very easy for him to make her giggle and blush.

"Come on, C. That's not fair. I want the rest of the story," Connor said in his best Paul Harvey voice. He slung an arm around her shoulders and rubbed the red jacket. "Hey, if only this jacket could talk, huh?"

"You know, Jax wore it to his audition on Saturday night," Celeste added.

"No way! He finally got an audition with that band? What's it called?" he asked, trying to remember.

"I don't know the name of it—some kind of fusion-rock band," Celeste said. "But Simone says he didn't get home until four in the morning. I guess he had to climb back into his house through a window so that his parents wouldn't hear the front door."

"That must've been some audition then!" Connor gasped. "So, is he in?"

"I don't know," Celeste answered. "I just know he came back at four." It was constantly amazing to her, the freedom all of her friends seemed to be able to enjoy at their leisure. *They want to do something and they just do it. No long lectures. No negotiating with multiple generations. No lengthy discussions and phone calls to aunts and uncles. What's it like to run free without the weight of your entire family's honor on your back? I'll probably never know.*

Connor rolled his eyes at her. He was slightly annoyed. "I guess I *should* be talking to Simone. You seem to have only incomplete information."

Celeste raised her hand up to him and turned her face away. "Talk to the hand, bro. You no like, I no talk to you," she said simply, trying not to laugh.

Connor sighed. "Actually, I'd rather talk to Andy—that beautiful man…" He glanced over at Celeste and smirked.

She burst out laughing. "He doesn't play on your team, Mister C. Better get over it."

"Well, if he won't have me, and if you don't end up living happily ever after with Tranh, the Vietnamese Wonder Boy, I'll marry you, okay? We'll have lots of beautiful half-breed babies," Connor said. He stopped the car in front of Celeste's house.

Celeste leaned in toward Connor so that she was inches from his face. "You're gay, Connor," she whispered. "I don't think that's going to happen," She winked and a smile crept across her face as she got out of the car. *Ha! We would have beautiful babies though. Wouldn't my family just love that…*

"Oh, yeah! Thanks for reminding me," he joked. "My family will be thrilled when I finally tell everyone." He smiled and pointed directly at Celeste before she shut the passenger side door. "Hey, make sure you call me tomorrow. I want to hear all about the big date with Tranh. Everything! Don't make me go to Simone for the details!"

"Okay," Celeste laughed. "Bye, Connor. Thanks for the ride!" Still giggling, she slammed the car door and hurried up the walk to her house. She knew her mother had been watching them closely through the window.

§§§§§

Tranh drove his uncle's SUV to pick up Celeste for their date. When he came to the door, she was pleasantly surprised that he was neither nerdy nor gawky. He wore jeans and a black leather jacket. His longish, silky black hair was brushed back from his face. He wore aviator sunglasses on top of his head, and his smile was sweet and genuine. A simple gold chain hung around his neck.

"You're not what I expected," she admitted to him as she buckled herself into the passenger seat.

Tranh grinned and looked over at her. "Violin virtuoso? Brilliant genius student? I didn't think you'd even talk to me," he replied. He smiled at her again. "And I didn't expect you to be so cute."

Celeste felt herself blushing. *This might not turn out to be so bad after all.* She smiled. "Please don't tell me that we're going bowling. Or that you're taking me to some Asian-American ice cream social at your grandma's church…"

"I wouldn't think of it," he said coolly.

"And I need to find a restroom before we get anywhere important," Celeste informed him. She began to mentally taken inventory of the collection of clothes she had in her large shoulder bag on her lap. *Too flashy? Too trashy? Wonderful. If we end up at a bingo game, I'm definitely rolling up my shirt and showing some skin.*

They stopped at a gas station to fill up the SUV, and Celeste got the key for the ladies' room, hoping it wouldn't be too filthy. Once inside, she finished up the makeup job she'd started at home, but always had to finish elsewhere. With aquamarine eye shadow, jet-black mascara, pink lipstick, and the lightest brush of sparkles on her neck and collarbone, she looked a lot more like Model C—her alter ego she had told Connor about.

She hastily stuffed her white blouse into her shoulder bag and carefully slid the glittery green spandex tank shirt over her head. She accessorized with silver earrings, a silver necklace, and four bracelets. The flat black shoes she had worn out of the house disappeared into her bag, too. They were quickly replaced by shiny black pumps with little green bows on the toes. It was hard to balance and switch the shoes without stepping onto the dirty floor, so Celeste put paper towels down all around her to be safe. Then she slipped on the charmingly oversized red jacket, and surveyed this final touch in the grimy mirror.

Trash! You look like trash! You bring shame to us, Celeste! You bring dishonor to your family after everything we have done for you. It is your duty to be a good girl—not trash like all of those American girls! You'll wind up pregnant, Celeste! You'll wind up arrested!

Grandma, they don't arrest you for getting pregnant.

Be quiet, Mama. I just want to have a little fun.

May I please just go out on one date without your voices in my head?

She left the ladies' room, and her cell phone rang as if on cue. With a sigh, Celeste flipped open her phone to take her mother's call, her face expressionless.

Celeste knew the almost-daily lecture in Vietnamese by heart: *You are not like the Americans! You will behave with decency! Vietnamese girls do not shame their families! It is about duty, respect, and honor.* She was not expected to answer, only to listen. In fact, it was better to just let her mother go on with her rant and then get off the phone, rather than try to argue, as her older sister did. Subservience, obedience, and respect. When Celeste bit her tongue, it got her mother off the phone a lot faster.

At least I can go on a date without three family members, like my cousin had to. That didn't seem to help; she ended up in a shotgun wedding. Another cousin had actually been sent back to Vietnam—a fate which hung over Celeste and made her shudder at the thought of it.

Back in the SUV, Tranh was waiting patiently. When Celeste helped herself in and buckled herself up, Tranh let out a low whistle of admiration. "You are really, *really* not what I expected, Celeste."

She tossed her hair and flashed a bright smile. "I'll take that as a compliment," she said. "So...tell me where we're going—wait! Don't tell me! Surprise me!" Her eyes sparkled, partly because of the makeup glitter on her lids and partly with genuine anticipation.

"Surprise you, huh? Well, I *did* have something in mind, but now I think we'll go somewhere else," he told her mysteriously as they drove away from the gas station. Tranh's shades were back on, so Celeste couldn't see his eyes. He was grinning at her though, and she found herself deciding that she really liked the sound of his voice. This was an interesting first—a date set up by her family with a guy she might actually like to see again...

"Okay," she answered, matter-of-factly. "But you're going to have to answer some questions first."

"What kind of questions?" he asked slowly.

"Hey! *I'm* asking the questions here!" Celeste cried. She settled herself into the seat, leaning toward Tranh. She tried to catch his eye behind the mirrored shades. "Your job is to answer *completely* and *truthfully,* okay?"

Tranh glanced at her as he drove; he couldn't help it—she was adorable. Her dark brown eyes were bright as she grinned at him, and she unconsciously shook her glossy black hair as it fell across her face. Tranh gripped the steering wheel a little more firmly as the urge to reach out and brush her hair from her cheek came over him.

"Oka—" Tranh cleared his throat as his voice had suddenly turned husky. "Okay, let me have it."

"What's your favorite color?" Celeste demanded.

"My favorite—well, somehow I thought these would be more difficult questions," he laughed.

"Just answer the question!" Celeste exclaimed.

"Brown!" *The color of your eyes. Deep brown satin, like a doe's eyes...*

"What's your favorite food?" she continued.

"I don't eat food," he said gravely, trying not to smile.

"Tranh!" Celeste erupted into giggles. "You're not answering *truthfully!*"

"Oh, sorry. Okay, um, Little Debbie Oatmeal Creme Pies," he replied, pretending to get all serious. "Please, continue. These questions are so...deep."

"What's your favorite band?" Celeste asked, ignoring his attempt to poke fun at her.

"No wait—Little Debbie *used* to be my favorite," Tranh blurted, correcting himself. "Now I think my favorite food is really chocolate cheesecake brownies."

"Tranh!" Celeste punched him on the shoulder.

"What?" he laughed. "With those little tiny chocolate chips? C'mon! They're to *die* for."

"You're not answering my question!" Celeste's giggles sounded like wind chimes in a summer breeze.

"Yes, I am," Tranh insisted. "Didn't you tell me I had to answer everything completely and truthfully? Well, I got confused about my favorite food. I had to clear it up."

"All right, all right," Celeste grinned, rolling her eyes. "Let's continue the interview. You're going to answer completely and truthfully, right?"

"Yes, ma'am," Tranh replied.

"Have you ever had a threesome?" Celeste asked without skipping a beat.

"*What!?*" Tranh blurted.

They dissolved into gales of laughter, and Tranh thought he might have to pull over to avoid an accident. Celeste's interview was thoroughly derailed, and they talked and laughed about nothing until they reached their destination.

Be quiet, Mama, I'm just having fun.

Tranh parked his SUV on the street at the end of a cul-de-sac. He took Celeste's hand as they walked up to a small house that desperately needed a paint job.

"What's happening here?" Celeste wanted to know.

"It's a surprise, right? You wanted to be surprised," Tranh reminded her.

"Oh, yeah..." she muttered. They stood on the front porch of the house and glanced at each other. They could hear loud music pulsing through the door. Tranh winked at Celeste and knocked.

I know there are probably lots of boys in there, Mama, and yes, I know they all want one thing. If you don't stop screeching at me, I may just go in there and join a threesome now.

"You never answered my question!" Celeste stood up on her toes and whispered in Tranh's ear right before the door opened. She gripped Tranh's hand tightly as she allowed herself to be led inside to a dark living room. A few people were dancing. Tranh introduced her to a couple of guys but she couldn't hear their names. Strange, sweet-smelling smoke made her eyes water, and she kept glancing at Tranh for reassurance that he would look after her. Unfortunately, he still had his mirrored shades on; she couldn't read his eyes.

The two of them found a couch in another room and decided to sit down. Celeste smiled, but her face started to ache as she tried to keep it up, like waiting for a picture to be taken as someone fiddled with the camera. This place was weird, and the music was harsh on her well-trained ears. She *had* asked for a surprise, but now she kind of wished that she and Tranh could be somewhere quieter—someplace where they could talk and get to know each other a little better, like they had been doing moments before.

Mama, it's okay. Don't worry about me. This is just about freedom and fun; it's not about family honor. I'm sorry you never had any fun, Mama.

Tranh had something in his hands. It was a glass contraption, like something from a mad scientist's laboratory. Smoke swirled around inside its bulblike section—ephemeral snakes coiling and gliding among themselves. Celeste started to get a headache. She looked at Tranh and winced, hoping he would understand that she was feeling slightly uncomfortable. Tranh just smiled back at her, oblivious. He placed the contraption to his lips and inhaled, sucking the smoke-serpents in. He held his breath for a few seconds and exhaled slowly. Then he offered the glass contraption to Celeste by touching her arm and nodding. She shivered in the red jacket and wondered if perhaps she should've listened to her parents this time.

Suddenly, she was somewhere else. It felt like she was standing in the same house but something about it had changed. Its windows had become eyes, and the doorways were now mouths—misshapen and trying to talk to her. It was all very sinister, filling her with an overwhelming sense of dread. She wanted to leave, but couldn't find a doorway that wasn't a mouth, leering at her, laughing at her. Finally, she found a window she could look out of. She leaned out with hopes of finding an escape, but realized that she was now perched on the edge of a cliff. At the bottom of the cliff was a group of people who were clustered around a small form. Everyone was crying.

No, the people weren't crying; they were wailing in grief. Celeste could hear the most heart-wrenching sobs, as if these people would never be happy again. They knelt over the tiny, unmoving form of a girl—a girl with black hair and a broken violin in her hands.

…It was her. Celeste was looking down at her own body, surrounded by her terror-stricken family—the people she loved most in the world.

"Celeste?" Tranh's voice cut through the strange vision and the loud music. "What's the matter? Haven't you done this before?"

She stared at his face but saw only her own reflection in his sunglasses. The image of her own body was replaced by her face and her brown eyes; the pretty makeup camouflaged her confusion. Wordlessly, she shook her head. She could hardly hear herself think with the pounding music and her mother's voice clamoring in her brain. *You want to be arrested? You want to give your mother heart attack?*

"Don't worry. I'll take care of you," Tranh whispered in her ear. For a moment, she thought it was the voices of the smoky snakes coiling inside the glass ball that had just spoken. She glanced at Tranh and nodded nervously. Taking the pipe, she leaned forward and carefully put her lips on it. She inhaled deeply as Tranh had done, and her mother's voice disappeared.

DAY EIGHTEEN

Simone was wearing the red jacket again. She had taken it out of its locker after school, and was headed over to the football field to meet Andy. They usually met up after practice, if Simone didn't have to pick up her brother or Andy wasn't working at his part-time job. *Once I sign a contract for $10 million,* he loved telling Simone, *I'm ditching the job! And buying a Ferrari.*

A red-haired girl from English composition class was walking in the other direction. Simone waved to her. The girl didn't respond, pretending she hadn't seen Simone's friendly gesture. She had stopped waving back a long time ago, when Simone first started going out with Andy. Simone shook it off. The redhead was just another girl with a crush on Andy who now didn't want to talk to her. *For God's sake, just put your big girl panties on and deal with it!* She tried not to let the whole thing bother her, but deep down it did. She was a sociable person and felt the alienation keenly.

A small frown furrowed Simone's brow as she slowed and scanned the field. She didn't see Andy anywhere. *Maybe he's already in the showers? That's odd though. He said he'd meet me on the field before he went in.*

A big guy in a football uniform started running at her. She stared, slightly confused and not wanting to get knocked over. *Ohmigod.* She hadn't recognized her own boyfriend. *What the heck did he do?*

"Andy!" Simone cried in astonishment, raising her hands in the air. "What happened to you?"

Andy grinned at her and shrugged. "What? Do I have something in my teeth?" he laughed.

Simone whacked him with her book bag. "You lunchbox! You shaved your *head!*"

"Oh. That. Yep…" he smiled slyly, running a large hand over his now bald and naked-looking pale scalp.

Simone stared at him, tears welling up in her eyes. "*Why?* Your hair was so *beautiful!*"

Andy glanced away uncomfortably. He hadn't expected her to react this way. The last thing he wanted was for her to get so upset. He knew how emotional she could get sometimes. He sighed and tried to make light of the situation. "Well, you know, what with all the curlers and blow-drying and seaweed conditioners and all, it was just too much to take care of," he answered. Simone didn't even crack a smile. She had adored his wavy, golden-brown locks. His hair was his signature trademark. It was part of the reason why all the guys were so jealous of him, and it made all the girls melt.

Simone stood with her hands on her hips, scowling at him.

"And you know my hairdresser, Raoul—the transvestite with the purple mohawk? He had to leave the country. Deported. Or maybe he was abducted by aliens. I had no choice but to shave it all off, babe," Andy added.

Simone wasn't buying it. "You could've *told* me," she muttered. "Or *warned* me is more like it."

"You wouldn't have wanted me to do it," he argued.

"You're right," she hissed.

Andy opened his arms wide. "Come on, Simone. Who do ya love?"

Simone sighed dramatically and allowed herself to be wrapped in his bear-hug embrace. "Just so you know, you look like something that's been buried and dug up again," she continued.

Simone experienced a strange sensation as she was pressed up against Andy's chest. Something was different about him, but what? He wasn't wearing his shoulder pads, so it couldn't be that. He just seemed softer somehow. *Is my boyfriend getting fat?*

Suddenly, Simone was watching Andy in the guys' locker room. It was right after practice and he was getting ready to shower. She wasn't sure why she was here, but she could see the whole team—some guys had their towels slung around their hips, some didn't have towels at all. Andy headed into the showers with a bar of soap and a large towel. He was careful to keep himself covered, and he stayed on the far end of the showers. It was obvious that he was trying to keep his back turned, almost as a shield, and he washed quickly. Some of the other guys called to him but Simone couldn't understand what they were saying. It was like they were speaking in another language. Andy scowled and shot back a retort, trading insults. He wrapped the towel around his hips again and stalked off to his locker. He seemed hurt or ashamed.

"Andy?" Simone looked up into his ocean-blue eyes.

The smile died on Andy's lips—Simone seemed to know something; she seemed to be looking right into him. He suddenly pushed her away.

"What?" he asked irritably. "It's just *hair,* for Pete's sake." He rolled his eyes and walked off toward the parking lot.

Surprised, Simone grabbed her book bag and hurried after him. "All right, I'm *sorry!* I just wasn't expecting it!" she apologized. She slipped her arm through his. "Aren't you going to the showers?"

"I'm showering at home," he muttered.

Simone's red leather-clad arm, snuggled inside Andy's elbow, tingled a little and she had a realization: *He doesn't want them to see him naked. In the locker room and the showers—he doesn't want them to see him.*

Andy stopped and turned to face Simone. He stared down at her arm. The memory of the cigarette, and the cloying, claustrophobic feeling of hospital beds and stale sweat assaulted him all over again. He hadn't had a cigarette since that dreadful experience. He shuddered and shook her arm from his.

"Andy? What's the matter?" Simone pleaded.

"Nothing," he responded. He was suddenly grouchy and just wanted to be left alone. "I just don't like that jacket. Why do you have to wear it *all* the time?"

"What?" Simone was confused. "You do too like this jacket! You're a co-owner." She shrugged and half-smiled at him with hopes that he'd smile back. No such luck.

"Yeah, well, I gotta go. I'll see you later," he said. He strode off toward the parking lot, leaving Simone mystified and standing on the lawn by herself. But as he walked away, she suddenly saw that one of the guys had written BITE ME on the back of Andy's shaved head with a black marker.

"I said I was sorry!" Simone called after him, and then turned away in disgust. *What on earth has gotten into him?* she wondered. *And why would one of his teammates write on the back of his head?* She didn't have any answers and decided to head home. Andy would call her when he was ready to talk—or so she hoped.

In the driver's seat of his car, Andy started the engine and then paused. He angled the rearview mirror so he could see his own reflection, and gingerly touched his receding hairline. This was the same hairline that had been completely normal three months ago, and he was not yet eighteen. Now it was clearly receding, with a balding patch developing on the crown of his head. It had been so alarming that Andy thought the only way to camouflage it was to shave it all off. However, what seemed like a good idea ended up backfiring. Now it just showed how far back his hairline had really withdrawn. And how fast.

§§§§§

Karen's cell phone rang and she glanced down at the screen. The incoming call was from SCUMBUCKET. She took a deep breath and flipped it open.

"Dudette!" Jax's voice announced happily.

"Hi, Jax," she said into the phone.

"Where are you?" Jax asked. He seemed eager.

"Home," she replied.

"Can you get away? Meet me at the Wishing Tree," Jax instructed.

There was a brief silence on Karen's end. Her eyes opened wide. "The *Wishing Tree?* Are you sure?"

Jax let out a burst of laughter. "Am I sure, she asks? Sure, I'm sure. Sure as God made little green apples. You bring the Cheez Whiz; I'll bring the crackers," he said.

"You did say to meet at the Wishing Tree, right?" Karen asked, hesitant.

Jax laughed again. "Is there an echo in here? I'll see you there in an hour, okay?"

"Okay," she agreed. Karen slowly closed her cell phone and stared at it for a moment. They'd known each other their whole lives yet she had never heard him this excited before. *What's going on?*

And now the moments she had been waiting for, for such a long time, seemed to be rushing in upon her. She was suddenly excited, confused, and a little annoyed with Jax's overzealous good mood. *I should take a lesson on happiness from him,* she thought. Lately though, no matter how hard she tried, she couldn't seem to lift her spirits. She could still maintain the illusion that someday the two of them could really happen—someday. But a small feeling of dread blossomed in the pit of Karen's stomach, knowing Jax had news she was sure she didn't want to hear. She took a deep breath and exhaled slowly. She was committed as his friend. She had to go see what was up.

Three years had passed since Karen and Jax had been to the Wishing Tree together. It was a mile-and-a-half away from their street, through the abandoned quarry, across the river, and through the sumac trees where nobody else could find the path but the two of them. At one point in time, it had once been a refuge for them when Karen's parents got divorced. It became a meeting place for the two of them when Jax's cousins decided they didn't want to play with him anymore because he was black. Karen and Jax had plotted revenge as they sat under the Wishing Tree's gnarled branches. They had laughed and cried together under that tree; they had dreamed the dreams of children. At sixteen, they had outgrown the Wishing Tree. Now they spent most of their time on the Internet and as Boogerhead and Scumbucket on their cell phones.

…But the Wishing Tree had one last role to fulfill.

"Well?" Karen demanded once they had reached the tree. "What is it?"

Jax had seated himself on a log and was digging through his backpack. "Do you want Cheez-Its or Triscuits?" he asked casually.

"Agh!" Karen groaned, grabbing the backpack away from him. "Let's have it! The whole story! You're *killing* me with the suspense!" she cried while pleading differently on the inside. *Please don't tell me this…*

Jax laughed and sprang up from the log. "How do you know I have a story?" he teased.

"Jax!" Karen punched him on the shoulder. "The last time we were here? Three years ago? Do I need to refresh your memory?" she asked, cracking a smile.

"Wait! Oh yeah, it's coming back to me now…" Jax interrupted her. He was still grinning. "We made a pact."

"*Yes*. And now you've dragged me out here," Karen prodded. "And I didn't come for the Cheez-Its!"

Jax continued smiling at his friend without saying a word. He truly savored torturing her this way. But it had been almost impossible to not share the big news with Karen the moment after it had happened. He took a dramatic breath before speaking. "Okay, so when we were thirteen, we agreed that when either of us lost our virginity, we would come out here and tell the other one about it," he explained slowly.

"Yes! Jax, I know! So spill the beans!" Karen exclaimed. Her heart was pounding.

"Well, her name is Jasmine," Jax grinned and paused. He paced back and forth under the tree. The energy in him animated his eyes and gave his slender limbs a cat-like grace.

Karen's heart pounded. *Jasmine.* A name made it real. It had happened. A maelstrom of emotions erupted in her gut. A rushing sound filled her head. Two seconds ago, when she hadn't known her name, she could still cling to the hope that it was a mistake; it hadn't really happened. *Jax, it was supposed to be you and me. It was always supposed to be you and me. I just tried to distract myself with David Steinberg, and that turned into a disaster.*

"She's the most beautiful woman I've ever met!" Jax burst forth, still in motion. He didn't notice the color draining from Karen's face. "She's older than me, but that doesn't matter. She's taking classes at the community college and playing with Seventh Heaven. She used to date Luke, the leader of the band, but they broke up. She has the most amazing eyes, Karen, and she loves my music!" He paused for a moment, his own eyes aglow with the recent memories of a life-changing experience.

He's back there with her, Karen realized. *He's remembering her, what it was like, everything. The most beautiful woman he's ever met...* Her own memories crowded in and threatened to make her head explode—the memories of her own experience she had been trying to avoid—and the bittersweet sense of loss as the love she felt for her friend throbbed like an open wound. It was apparent now that Jax, her best friend and soulmate, would never see her as anything more than Boogerhead.

Jax continued. He was on a roll. "I can't even tell you what it was like!" he exclaimed. His face was dreamy, revealing that it had been an experience beyond words.

Thank God for that, Karen thought desperately. She just smiled as he spoke, still wanting him to go on and wanting him to stop at the same time.

"So, we went to her apartment. She asked me to sing some of my songs. At first I was a little hesitant, but then I realized she was genuinely interested, you know? She really *heard* the lyrics and everything. She really got what my music is about!" he said, his voice speeding up. "And once we got inside? *Oh man,* Karen..." Jax was about to let out a whistle for added emphasis when a choked sob finally got his attention. He stopped pacing. "Karen?"

Her face was red and tears streamed down her cheeks.

"Karen!" Jax put his arm around her shoulders and gently sat her down on the log. "What's the matter? What's wrong?" Her body shook with sobs and her nose began to run.

"I—I—" she started, but could barely get the words out.

"What? Tell me!" Jax encouraged, holding her by the shoulders.

She turned her swollen, tear-streaked face to him. "I'm—happy—for you," she finally managed to say.

"What? Karen, something's obviously upsetting you! What is it?" he demanded.

"It's not just you," Karen whispered. She took a deep breath. "We both lost our virginity."

"What? Really? Well, that's great!" Jax leaned close to her red face. "Isn't it? Aren't you happy?"

Karen sighed and shook her head. "I thought it was supposed to be great. It was supposed to be a turning point, you know?" she asked, feeling crushed. She looked into Jax's warm brown eyes, full of concern. She managed a rueful smile. "Anyway, it was my own fault. I was drunk at Melina's party—"

"David! Was that guy, David, there?" Jax's expression suddenly darkened. "Was he mean to you? Did he hurt you?"

"No, I mean yes—David was there, but he has a girlfriend. It was Glen," Karen said softly. Just saying his name aloud gave her chills.

"Glen? Who's Glen?" Jax wondered. He thought it was strange that Karen had never mentioned him before.

She sighed again and wiped her face with her hands. "He's Melina's brother's friend. He's twenty-eight. He was hanging out with her brother and showed up at the party," she muttered.

"And you met him how?" Jax asked skeptically.

"I was sitting outside, blubbering my eyes out kind of just like now, she tried to laugh between sobs. "He felt sorry for me, I guess. He took me for a ride…"

"…*And?*" Jax prodded.

"And what?" Karen snapped a little. "I was drunk. I was a mess. He wanted to 'comfort' me. I'm pretty sure you can guess the rest."

Jax stared at his friend, speechless. The self-loathing on Karen's face twisted his heart. He wanted so much to take the beauty and exhilaration which was filling him up and share it with her, to somehow try and erase her pain and shame. He wasn't exactly sure what to say. "So, did you *want* to do it?" he finally asked after a few moments of silence.

"I don't know," Karen buried her face in her hands. "I wanted to do it with David." *I wanted to do it with you, but that's never going to happen.* "I was too drunk to really stop him, and it just happened."

"Karen," Jax lifted her face with one hand. He looked directly into her tear-filled eyes. "Did he rape you?"

"No. It wasn't that," she said quickly. "It just wasn't what I really wanted." Her voice dropped to a whisper. "It was supposed to be beautiful."

Jax suddenly saw something raw and unguarded in her eyes. He finally had to glance away. "Karen, did he use a condom?" he asked bluntly.

"Did you?" she asked back.

As they sat beneath the Wishing Tree, the silence between them answered both questions.

DAY TWENTY-SIX

"Celeste, what's the combination?" Connor rattled the lock as he spoke into his cell phone.

Giggles came out of the earpiece and Connor rolled his eyes. "Don't tell me you forgot it," Celeste said playfully.

"If I could remember it, do you think I would be calling you right now and asking for the combination?" Connor asked.

More giggles. "I'm almost there. Don't have a conniption. I'll open it for you," Celeste replied.

The line went dead. Connor leaned up against the locker where the red jacket was kept and ran his hands through his hair. He always did this when he was nervous. He also started shifting his weight from one foot to the other. *What's taking her so long?* It was finally Connor's turn to wear the jacket, and for the love of God he couldn't remember the stupid combination.

He also hadn't been able to eat breakfast or lunch today; his stomach was too uneasy. When he woke up in the morning, it had seemed like any other ordinary day. But today would mark a turning point—the day he came into being. Today was the day he would tell his parents. It had to be today; he couldn't wait any longer. The stress of his parents not knowing who he was had finally outweighed the stress of what would happen when he told them.

A poster at his family's church kept reappearing in his mind as he waited impatiently for Celeste to show up. TODAY IS THE FIRST DAY OF THE REST OF YOUR LIFE, the poster's sentiment intoned. It was banal and silly, somehow, but true. Connor's life would from now on consist of a *before* and an *after*. He felt confident that, once his parents got over their initial shock, they would understand and re-adjust. And then Connor would be looked upon as an *adult*. He wasn't a confused kid. He knew who he was and had known for quite some time now. But it was finally time for other people—the most important people in the world to him—to know who he was, too.

Up until today, the internal conflict he had been dealing with had been building and spiraling out of control for years. He had experienced powerful feelings of desire, shame, guilt, and inadequacy all at the same time. He had wondered if something was wrong with him because he had never been attracted to girls. He had no idea how he had become this way, only that he couldn't remember ever feeling anything else. His earliest memories of sexual attraction had always been toward other boys—never to a girl—although he had tried imagining himself with a girl. Celeste was his closest friend, and he had tried imagining kissing her, but it held nothing for him. He just couldn't think of her, or any other girl for that matter, in *that* way.

Andy, on the other hand, with his large, athletic body, always got his attention, causing maelstroms of desire from within. He had to hide it, *always*. And with Jax—sensitive, beautiful, complex, with the most amazing velvet eyes, the color of spice and sunlight—Connor had to force himself to look away otherwise he'd be overwhelmed.

Hanging out with Celeste was safe. People assumed all kinds of things about the two of them, but being with her was straightforward. He didn't have to worry about crazy confusion or desires so strong he couldn't hear himself think. He knew Celeste's parents were nervous about him—wanting her to eventually marry a Vietnamese guy—and worried that she might even want to end up with him. *That* was not going to happen in this lifetime. In fact, their daughter was safer with him than with just about anyone else. Celeste was like a sister to Connor.

"Finally! It took you long enough," Connor grumbled as he saw Celeste approaching.

She grinned and stuck a folded-up piece of paper in his hand. "Read it, memorize it, destroy it. Got it?" she grinned. It was, of course, the combination to the red jacket's locker. "We already gave you this weeks ago!"

"Well, I forgot. Sue me. I haven't taken it out yet," Connor snapped. He felt on edge.

"Why are you so grumpy today?" Celeste asked, rolling her eyes. She had the lock open in an instant and took the jacket out. She looked up at Connor's face and saw his pensive expression. She always loved looking at his sweet face; he always looked innocent and a little shy. But today it was apparent that something was weighing heavily on him. *Ohmigod*. Instantly, it came to her. "Connor!" she whispered theatrically, grabbing his arm. "Is this it? Are you doing it *today?*"

"Shhh!" Connor hissed back at her, taking the jacket. "Don't announce it to the whole world!"

"Come on. Let's go outside," Celeste said. She slammed the locker shut and dragged Connor along with her. They walked out across the front lawn in silence.

When they were away from any potential eavesdroppers, Celeste spoke up. "Well, what are you gonna say to them? Do you think they have an idea? Maybe they already know that something is up," Celeste suggested.

Connor shook his head. "I don't think they have any idea. My folks seem to think I'm still ten years old. That's how they treat me, anyway." He sighed at the thought of them still babying him.

"But what are you going to *say?*" Celeste was dying to know.

Connor shrugged. He sighed and ran his hand through his hair again. "I just want them to *know* me, Celeste. I want them to know *me*—who I really am. I don't want to keep such a big secret. It also feels like I can't grow up in their eyes if they keep thinking I'm some ten-year-old who only ever thinks about stamp collections and—"

"Interior decorating? Window treatments?" Celeste offered with a smile.

Connor slung a hand on one hip and made a half-turn, his body shifting with a dancer's grace into a silly pose. He affected a bored expression and a lisp. "Honey, I just cannot *believe* you are using the tulle and not the organdy. I mean, really, that's just so *last year!*" he joked.

Celeste grabbed his hand and lifted it, making it wobble at the wrist. "Do this! Here, do this…"

Connor snatched his hand away and they both burst into laughter. He wrapped one leather-clad arm around her small shoulders. "You witch! You think that's a good approach, huh?"

"Nah," she said, turning serious. She looked into his eyes and smiled. "Just be yourself."

The red jacket's scent, warming in the sunlight, filled Celeste's head, making her think of new car seats and warm rain after a winter thaw. She was grateful for this moment; she was grateful for her friendship with Connor.

Suddenly, she envisioned herself inside Connor's house, and his parents were shouting at him. They had tears in their eyes. The ferocity of their expressions stunned Celeste. She was horrified.

Celeste slipped her arms around his waist, hugging him tightly. Tears pricked at her eyes, and she hid her face, not wanting him to see. "I still love you, Connor, no matter what happens."

Connor was shocked into silence, but quickly recovered. "Well, sure, Celeste—Miss C, you're my best friend." He peeled her arms from his body and looked into her sharp dark-brown eyes, eyes that never missed a thing. "It's going to be *fine*."

He walked her out to the car to drive her home, with an arm slung companionably around her shoulder. "*You,* young lady, have not spilled the beans about the big date! You know, with Tranh, the Vietnamese Paragon? How was it? What did you do? Was there tongue involved?" he asked, chuckling.

"*Connor!*" Celeste squealed. A fluttery feeling entered the pit of her stomach; she actually couldn't remember very much about the date.

"Was he a nerd? Was he a rock star? Am I going to have to beat you senseless to get the whole story?" Connor continued.

Celeste thought for a moment. "He was—he was, well, let's just say...not what I expected. He was pretty cool, actually. He's a sophomore in college. He's studying philosophy. Basically, we had a great time," she said with a shrug.

"A great time? Do you mean like a great time or a *great time?*" Connor pushed.

Celeste laughed again. "Jeez, Connor, do you ever think about anything else?"

"Not really. Should I get the shotgun out to defend your honor?" he continued.

"Oh, *now* you're all worried about my honor! Well, my honor is fine, thank you very much. You better worry about your own, homeboy. You have big plans for the red jacket tonight," Celeste smiled, adding coyly, "You look stunning, by the way."

Connor felt his face flush a little. He grinned at the compliment. "Big plans, yeah. I'm going out after, you know..."

Celeste's heart quickened. *After the big scene with his parents,* she thought. She felt uneasy. She didn't want her friend to get hurt in the process of telling his parents what he was about to tell them. She thought fast. "Connor, are you sure this is a good idea? Maybe this isn't the best time," she suggested right as he pulled up in front of her house. She was no longer laughing.

"Don't worry, Model C," he smiled, but the smile didn't reach his eyes, which were clouded over with anxiety. "It will be okay. I mean, I have to tell them sometime."

§ § § § §

Connor parked his dad's car in the driveway and walked up to the side door, pausing with his hand on the doorknob. He had spent an hour-and-a-half driving around aimlessly since dropping Celeste off at her house, trying to collect his thoughts and the perfect words to tell his parents. Now he was at the tan house on Maplewind Drive—the one in the middle of the block with the hedge of primroses out front—his home.

This was where Connor had grown up. He had literally been born and raised in this house, arriving a little sooner than expected after a difficult pregnancy for his mother, and he had been born in the living room while his parents had waited anxiously for the ambulance to arrive. His father and a neighbor lady had been there, and luckily it had all turned out okay. In fact, the story of how Connor made his big debut into the world on the living room carpet (which ultimately got ruined) became somewhat of a family legend. Whenever Connor's father recalled the story, he'd tell listeners about how Connor had also spit in his eye at only two minutes old. Connor would just smile sheepishly and shrug before everyone inevitably broke out into fits of laughter.

He meant to open the door and walk inside, but still paused with his hand gripping the knob. *How many times have I walked through this door?* They rarely used the front door of the house, but this one—this side entry into the sunlit kitchen and the breezeway where he and his brother had to take off their boots; where he had come rushing in with a bloody nose after Brendan from down the street had punched him; where he had opened the letter that held his first driver's permit—*this* door had been his portal to the world for nearly seventeen years.

If he couldn't walk through this door into his own home, the home that had raised and nurtured him for his whole life as who he really was, then it wasn't really a home, was it? These were his *parents*. They loved him. More importantly, they needed to know. Connor turned the knob and pulled, and as the edge of the door brushed the shoulder of the jacket, he had an odd thought.

His father was in his bedroom, yanking Connor's dresser drawers out and dumping their contents onto the floor. There were tears in his eyes and he looked furious, horrified, and full of rage. His mother stood by, wringing her hands and weeping uncontrollably. She tried to talk to his father, but he wouldn't listen. His father moved to the closet, tearing clothes from their hangers and hurling them out onto the floor with the rest of Connor's stuff.

Connor took a deep breath, steeled himself for what was to come, and walked slowly inside, shaking his head as if to clear it from the unsettling images. "Mom? Dad?" he called out uncertainly.

"Well, there you are!" Connor's mother, Janice, called to him from the living room. "You missed dinner." She was in her favorite chair in the family room, crocheting a sweater. *Wheel of Fortune* was on TV, with the sound down low so that it wouldn't bother John, his dad, as he read through legal briefs he had brought home from work.

Connor slowly walked into the family room and stood in front of the TV.

Janice looked up. "Hi, honey. Did you have a late orchestra rehearsal? There are leftovers in the fridge. Beef stroganoff," she said. She looked down again to focus on her sweater.

Connor picked up the TV remote from the end table next to his mother's chair and hesitated a second. Then he turned the TV off.

"Can I talk to you guys? About something?" he asked, still standing in front of them. John glanced up from his papers, at first slightly annoyed, but then alert and guarded, as he always was in the courtroom. As a litigator, his whole career was based on reading people and figuring out their motives and agendas, and his son clearly had an agenda tonight. He put his papers down and took off his bifocals.

"Have a seat, son," John motioned to the couch. It was his attempt to make Connor more comfortable, but it was also a standard procedure—never let anyone push the power balance by standing over you.

Connor sat carefully on the edge of the couch, unable to make himself relax. *Just breathe.*

"Where'd you get that jacket?" Janice asked curiously. "I've never seen it before."

"It's Simone's," Connor said slowly, as if sleepwalking. Words would only come to him one at a time, not in complete sentences, and he found himself having to hunt for them. "She loaned it...to me."

Connor's father was on full alert now. Years in the courtroom, in cross-examination, in board rooms, and on the street had primed him for all the signals—someone with something to hide, the guilty conscience, the confession about to burst forth. But his own *son?* What disaster was he about to drop on them? He braced himself for the worst.

"What's on your mind, Connor?" he tried to ask casually, his face guarded. Warning bells were going off at high volumes around him. *Drugs? It has to be drugs,* John immediately concluded in his mind. *Kids have access to everything these days: prescription meds, hard stuff, cocaine, meth, acid, everything. Connor's a smart kid, but maybe he has been hanging around with the wrong people? Who are his friends these days anyway? The little Chinese girl? Celeste? I think that's what her name is...*

Suddenly John felt out of the loop—out of touch with his younger son. A surge of parental protection welled up inside him. He glanced at his wife before speaking. "Listen, Connor. If you're having a problem, a little pot or something—" he started off. *Please, God, let it just be a little marijuana. That's a no-brainer; I could get him off of that pretty easily. But wait, wouldn't I have known about an arrest? Connor's still underage. We would've been notified...*

Connor stood up. "It's not that, Dad. It's not drugs," he said quickly.

John could feel his body suddenly get tense. *Standing up? That's not good. Never allow your respondent to stand over you. And when did the boy get so tall? For chrissake, he has to be at least six foot two now. He's taller than me! How did all of this happen? He's still a kid, for cryin' out loud.*

"What's the matter, Connor?" Janice asked. Her eyes were full of concern. "Just tell us what's going on."

A pregnancy! That must be it, John thought with inner relief. His mind was reeling, but still his face gave nothing away. *Did he knock up the little Chinese girl? Well, that wasn't the end of the world. These things could be taken care of...*

"Listen, son. If it's Celeste, if you've gotten her in trouble, well...ah, we can..." John offered awkwardly. *Can what? Help you arrange an abortion?* It was rare that the master litigator was at a loss for words. It was obvious to everyone in the room that John felt uncomfortable. He wondered if he should stand, too, to be at the same level as his son.

Connor looked down at his father. He wasn't exactly sure what he had been talking about with Celeste, but then it clicked. "What? Oh, no! It's nothing like that."

"It's okay, Connor. You can tell us," Janice piped up. "Celeste is a sweet girl but people do make mistakes, it's only natural—" She smiled warmly, hoping it would help.

"No, Mom!" Connor interjected. They were *really* off-track. *How will they know unless I speak up? I have to tell them now. I have to find the words and the courage right now.* He was drawing a blank. The words he had practiced in the car were all jumbled up inside of his head.

John stood up; he couldn't take the suspense anymore. Even on two feet, he was still looking up at his tall son. "We can handle this, Connor. We're here for you. We can get through this, I promise. I can call—"

"I'm gay! Dad, I'm gay," Connor blurted. "That's it. That's what I had to tell you. I'm—I'm…gay." *Sheesh. Here I am, trying to impress my parents by talking to them as an adult with a real identity, yet I'm coming across as a three-year-old.* He realized he had closed his eyes after he said the words. Slowly, he opened them back up.

His parents appeared frozen in a state of shock. Connor did his best to recover and fill the awkward silence with some kind of explanation—as if he telling them how he had accidentally broken the lamp in the hallway. "I just wanted you to know. You know, because, well, I love you," he said. Panic was rising in his voice. It started to crack. "I just wanted you to know." His practiced speech about people and life and love and who we all are to each other had vanished—gone from his mind.

Connor looked from his father's icy face to his mother, who still appeared shocked. "Mom?" he encouraged her to speak. She looked like she wanted to, but like Connor, couldn't find the right words.

"*Gay?*" she demanded. "How can that *be?*" Her face crumpled into confusion. Connor's heart contracted; he hadn't meant to cause them pain.

"It's just who I am, Mom," he said as he knelt down in front of her chair. "There's nothing wrong with me. You didn't do anything wrong. It's *okay*," He hoped she wouldn't cry. He hated to see his mother cry. But it happened anyway. Giant tears welled up and started rolling down her cheeks.

Then John spoke solemnly. "I would rather have a dead son than a gay son."

Connor stood back up and stared at him in amazement. He had never heard his father's voice like this—so cold, so utterly unfamiliar, so *bitter.*

"You—you're saying you would rather…have me *dead?*" Connor couldn't believe the words he had just uttered. His own father? His dad who had carried him on his shoulders, who had played the leapfrog game with him, who had watched hockey on TV with him and his brother on the couch, eating potato chips and peanut butter cookies? His own father who had carried him in his arms to the hospital when he had fallen out of a tree when he was six years old?

"I would rather have a dead son than a gay son," John repeated, his eyes as cold as ice. He turned and strode out of the room toward the stairwell. Janice immediately followed, pleading with him the entire time.

"John, wait! There's been some mistake, I'm sure. It's all a mistake. I'm sure there's some kind of explanation—something that can be done to fix this!" she called after him. He ignored her and stomped up the stairs. He was on a mission. Janice ran after him, begging him to calm down.

Connor stood glued to the floor, unable to move. *I know where he's going. I know what he's doing.* The sounds of the drawers being yanked from the dresser confirmed it. *I knew this; I saw it happening. They don't want me. I knew they would be disappointed, but this? They don't want me anymore? My dad wants me…dead?*

In a daze, Connor walked mechanically to the side door—the one he'd come through just a short time ago. It was the door he had walked through so many times as a boy, when his life was simple and carefree. He glanced at the car keys on the kitchen table, but then decided to leave them there. It wasn't his car. They weren't his keys.

Connor walked back out the side door and into the night. He had entered it as a boy, but now he left as…something else. He wasn't so sure anymore. However, one thing was certain: He'd have to keep moving. He'd have to get away from this place and from the family who no longer wanted him. He had to keep moving to find out who he was.

DAY TWENTY-SEVEN

It took two hours for Connor to walk to the south side of town. He could have taken a bus, but the nervous energy stampeding inside him needed time and activity. He felt many paradoxical emotions: he sought company but craved solitude; one minute he wanted to turn around and rush back home, telling his parents it was all a mistake; and at the same time he knew the so-called damage had been done. He could never go back. Several times he flipped open his cell phone to call someone, then snapped it shut again. He couldn't imagine getting onto a crowded bus with all of those other people, not with these emotions bursting inside him. Yet, he saw himself eagerly talking with the other passengers, reaching out to them, needing some kind of human interaction even if they were complete strangers: *Do you have a gay son or a gay brother? What did you do when you found out? Did you treat him like a monster the way my parents treated me?*

Finally his stomach reminded him that he hadn't eaten anything all day. A convenience store appeared in front of him—a mass of neon lights and fluorescent-painted signs hung in the windows. A homeless man, scruffy and tattered, leaned on the wall outside the door and held out a can. A paper sign taped to it simply read: PLEASE HELP.

"Hey, man," said the bum, looking up at Connor. "Got something for me?" He was wearing an old knit cap with earflaps pulled down low, framing a scraggly brown beard that was streaked with gray. His skin was sallow, his eyes were bloodshot, and he appeared to be in his late fifties or early sixties. He gently touched Connor's elbow, still clad in the red jacket, as he held out his can with the other hand. "Please?"

He's not as old as he looks. He's forty-eight years old, has been divorced twice, and hasn't seen his children in more than twelve years. They were the only ones he ever cared about. He sometimes lives in a dry culvert, sometimes in the park, and sometimes in the men's shelter when the weather's really bad. He goes by the name Izrael Hands, but that's not what had been listed on his driver's license years ago. He had a college education—he received a Master's degree in literature—and a white-collar job for a while. But bipolar disorder, alcoholism, and finally an addiction to methamphetamines eroded the man, devouring him like a cancer, and leaving only this shell in cast-off clothing. It usually takes a week of begging and panhandling to make enough for his next fix.

Connor gasped and stared at the man, unbalanced by this shocking clarity. It was as if the man's entire lifetime had been compressed into a single vivid moment and presented to Connor as an unwanted revelation. The moment dissolved when Connor suddenly backed up, jerking his arm away from Izrael Hands.

Too surprised to say anything, Connor made his way through the door and into the convenience store. *Izrael Hands? From the book,* Treasure Island, *but spelled differently? How do I know all this? What the hell?*

A few minutes later, Connor emerged from the store with a paper bag and two Cokes. He handed one to Izrael, who looked at it and nodded.

"You bought me this because you think I'll blow money on junk," Izrael said. He was simply making a statement, neither accusing nor cajoling. Connor reached into the bag, pulled out a tuna salad sandwich, and gave it to him. Izrael had to hold his can under one arm to take it. "And this is because I haven't eaten any solid food in two days," he added. His bloodshot eyes looked into Connor's and showed emotion—a mixture of gratitude and embarrassment. Izrael was still aware of who he was, from where he had come, and how far. "The name's Izrael—Izrael Hands. Thanks, man."

Connor took another tuna sandwich out of the bag and unwrapped it as fast as he could. He was ravenous, and this was as good a place as any to eat it. At least he had someone to talk to.

After the two of them ate quietly for a few minutes, Connor spoke up. "So, why Izrael Hands?" he asked between bites.

Izrael took a slug of Coke and looked at Connor. "A fantasy man on a fantasy island, I suppose, but more real than Bernard Schenkewitz ever was. Altered slightly, S to Z, because he's damaged goods. We're all damaged goods," he explained. He stuck out his weathered hand toward Conner. "It's a pleasure to make your acquaintance."

Connor shook his hand. "Connor," he said with a half smile. "Damaged goods as well." A sense of emptiness enveloped him. Curious, he nonchalantly rubbed the cuff of the red jacket against Izrael's arm and waited for something to happen. His heart pounded; he hoped Izrael didn't think something was up. Nothing. Just the two of them eating sandwiches on a mostly deserted sidewalk.

"You know what the worst part of it was?" Connor asked him, realizing he did want to talk about what had happened. He took another bite of his sandwich.

"What's that?" Izrael wondered, focusing on his own.

"The worst part of it was that my mom—*my own mother*—wouldn't stand up for me," Connor muttered, shaking his head. The homeless man nodded sympathetically. Connor continued. "She tried to make out like it was all a mistake, like I could be—fixed! You know, like taking a dog to the vet, for chrissake! She thinks there's something *wrong* with me."

Izrael sighed. "There's something wrong with everyone. Mothers, fathers, acrobats, even the guy—that guy, you know? The one with the red—the red thing?" He appeared confused, trying to focus on thoughts that eluded him. "But it's never what people say it is. Other people, you know, they think—they think they know what's wrong, and they just have their own things. They try to, you know, make *you* the reason for their own—damn, what's the word?" Izrael frowned and stopped eating for a moment, frustrated that his brain could no longer keep up with his thoughts.

Connor nodded. "I know what you're saying," he offered. He turned his thoughts back to his own situation. "I mean, she could have said something, *anything*. She could have stuck up for me."

"Inadvertently?" Izrael shook his head, as if trying to rattle his brain into cooperation.

"Izrael, she didn't even try to get me to stay there. Her own kid! She just let me walk out of the house," Connor exclaimed. He could feel his cheeks getting hot with anger.

"Inexcusable?" Izrael asked.

"And what kind of dad wishes for his own son to be *dead?*" Connor continued.

"Inadequacies!" Triumphant, Izrael had found the elusive word in the jumbled attic of his mind. "People and their *inadequacies!* They pretend it's really you and not them!"

Connor stared at him and grinned. "I think you're right. I thought that coming out to them would make me an adult, but becoming an adult is really when you see your own parents' inadequacies," he said. A disturbing thought clutched at him. "They can't protect me anymore. They're afraid and don't know what to do." *That must be it. I cannot believe he would really want me dead.* But the words still stung, lingering inside him with no way out.

Izrael finished his sandwich, took a swig of his Coke, and belched loudly. He glanced at Connor for a reaction, but he didn't get one. Connor was still concentrating on his problems. Izrael watched him try to figure things out. He found Connor rather interesting with all of his insight beyond his years.

"But now..." Connor sighed. "What now?" He felt like a small boy in spite of his huge frame. "Who is my family now? Who am *I* going to be?" He leaned closer to Izrael, and discovered that the man had not had the luxury of bathing in what smelled like quite some time. "How do *you* do it?"

"Oh, I'm a Toltec shaman," Izrael replied. "I follow the way of the Wise Ones." His demeanor shifted in a subtle way; a moment before he had looked deflated, a bit of human detritus washed up on a cracked sidewalk. But now the Toltec shaman asserted himself, standing taller and speaking with a quiet authority, with a light of intelligence finding its way out of his confused mind.

"A what? A Toltec what?" Connor asked. He couldn't tell if Izrael was being truthful or if he was about to go off on a crazy rant.

"Toltec shaman. We have been here for all of eternity," Izrael explained matter-of-factly. He took another sip of his soda. "We are the Wise Ones, the learned healers, those who carry on the tradition of knowledge."

"What kind of knowledge?" Connor asked. He was intrigued.

Izrael looked at Connor with watery blue eyes. They suddenly seemed clear and lucid. "Ancient knowledge—the voices of the Universe. There are those who fear this knowledge, so we have to go underground. We are a threat to those in power, so they try to kill us, to silence our voices, our knowledge," he said. His eyes grew wide and he glanced around to make sure no one was trying to eavesdrop. "So we disguise ourselves, and move through the world undetected. But we are here, and we carry on our tradition of seeking and knowing. We pass our great secrets on to those who know how to listen."

"What kind of secrets?" Connor wanted to know.

Izrael stared hard at Connor, evaluating him. *Is this boy worthy of the valuable knowledge I possess?* he wondered with caution. *It can't be passed out randomly to just anyone.* He decided Connor could be let in on the secrets. "Real wisdom," he finally answered. "It's the essence of humanity, untarnished by the meaningless obsession with self-delusion and neurotic self-absorption that unfortunately consumes us all."

Connor paused to consider this. *Self-delusion? Self-absorption? Maybe I am self-absorbed. Am I self-deluded? No, that's what I'm coming out of—I'm emerging from the state of delusion in which I've grown up.* "How does someone get to this knowledge, this 'essence of humanity'?" he asked.

Izrael finished his soda and tossed the can aside. He looked pensive. The spiritual being beside Connor could not completely separate from the physical need for sustenance. Connor pulled a bag of chips out of the paper bag and handed it to him. Izrael nodded with appreciation and continued.

"By following the eleven ways," he replied. Bits of potato chips flew out of his mouth. "The most important step—the first of the eleven ways—is the erasing of one's personal history." A few chip crumbs got caught in his scraggly beard. "Our modern technological culture is obsessed with the details of each other's lives. We're compulsively preoccupied with each other's life chronology, personal data, sexual and legal history, beliefs, religious views—all kinds of irrelevant details."

Izrael's eyes burned fiercely. Suddenly, he seemed like a different person. "We worship an illusion; we're drowning in our own self-importance. So we practice the art of cord-cutting: We disentangle ourselves from the illusion by erasing our personal history."

Connor considered Izrael's words carefully. *Cord-cutting? Making a break with a painful past? What if a person could recreate the present into something more manageable, less painful, and more real?* He wanted to hear more. "Okay, so how exactly does a person do the 'cord-cutting'?" he asked. *What if the events of today—the worst day of my life—had happened to someone else?*

"You must disentangle yourself with your personal history. Change your name, change your appearance, and change your address. Stop using words like 'I,' 'me,' and 'myself.' This frees up your mind for a greater awareness. Get rid of all the things that keep you rooted in the past—photos, memorabilia, possessions. In fact, stop letting people take photos of you altogether. Stop talking about your past, age, culture, any degrees you may have earned, past jobs, titles—all of that," Izrael spouted off. He stared at Connor to make sure he was still listening.

"Go on…" Connor urged.

"Don't reinforce the illusion. You break away from the slavery of the past and live in the only real moment, which is now. Stop explaining all your comings and goings to others. Their expectations will imprison your energy," Izrael explained. He paused, and his gaze shifted from Connor to a spot off to his left.

Connor watched him uncomfortably. Izrael seemed to be intent on something, nodding his head slightly as if listening to someone; his eyes were bright and focused. Connor glanced to the side to see that there was nothing there, and realized that Izrael was seeing someone who didn't exist.

"Izrael?" Connor asked him. "Hello?" He wondered if he should get going. To where though? He wasn't quite sure.

Once again Izrael was an old man, beaten down and deflated. Connor could almost see the energy leaving him, rendering him small and hollow, with a dull glaze to his eyes that had been so animated and alive moments before.

"Spare some change, man?" Izrael asked hesitantly, apparently having forgotten everything from the past half hour.

Connor stared at him, and slowly handed over the paper bag from the convenience store. There was still a package of cupcakes inside. Izrael took the paper bag and peered inside of it. "You bought me this because you think I'll blow money on junk," he said.

"Take care of yourself," Connor responded slowly. He stuck his hands in the pockets of the red jacket and began walking down the street.

An hour later, a light rain forced Connor to find shelter under a culvert overhang. A small pool of stagnant water had accumulated bits of garbage, leaves, and detritus where he first entered the makeshift shelter, but he eventually found a place that was dry and relatively clean to sit.

His face was wet from the rain, and the warm tears mixed with cool droplets on his skin. Once begun, the tears poured out like a river, releasing a flood of pain that seemed to arise from deep inside his gut, a place he didn't know existed. His body shook with sobs, and he wrapped his arms tightly around himself, as if to give himself comfort where he could find none. The image of his father's cold face and his unbelievable declaration would not leave him, running like an endless loop in his head. He also kept imagining his mother's averted gaze. *She couldn't even look at me...*

He wrapped his arms around himself tighter. *What have I done? Who am I now? Where am I going to go?* He couldn't stand the thought of returning to his home, the home of his childhood, to get his things. Maybe one of his friends could go over and pick up his stuff? But wasn't he supposed to be done with all of that—past relationships and the tangled web of his personal history? Wasn't the point of cord-cutting to sever *all* ties?

The idea had a bittersweet appeal: to become someone wholly new, unconnected to who he was before, leaving the pain and confusion of the old Connor behind. The thought was tantalizing. He imagined himself emerging like a butterfly from its chrysalis, changed from its juvenile form, transformed into a thing of beauty.

He flipped open his cell phone and scrolled through his list of phone numbers, deleting every single one in a series of blips. Tears obscured his vision so that he could not see friend after friend dissolving into oblivion. *Cord-cutting. Letting go of the past. It has to be done.*

Finally, he fell into an exhausted, uncomfortable, fitful doze, turning up the collar of the red jacket and pulling it close around him. He folded his arms tightly across his chest and hunched down into himself. He was an incubating butterfly, now gestating inside his cocoon of soft red leather, having cut the cords that tied him to the past.

Dreams carried him from the rainy culvert into the night, flying like the beautiful butterfly he was to become, and he saw into his friends' lives with crystal clarity. Celeste, closest to his heart, sweet and complex and funny and talented, imprisoned in her own personal history. Connor saw her with Tranh. Her eyes were bright and her laughter was brittle. She was taking something he gave to her, a smoking stick, or was it a snake? Celeste put her rosebud lips to it and inhaled the smoke. Instantly, Connor felt her exhilaration, her fear, her nervous excitement, and trepidation. He understood that she liked Tranh because he made her feel different, older, and more sophisticated. Yet, Connor could see that she was also terrified. She was afraid he wouldn't like her if she didn't do the things he did—things she would never have done on her own, like inhaling the poisonous snake-like smoke into her lungs. Connor could not speak to her; she could not see or hear him. He spread his filamentous wings and flew off.

Andy was in someone's car, sitting in the back seat. He took off his shirt, and Connor saw that he was well-muscled; he must've been working out. But his chest looked unusual, like a woman—prominent breasts on an otherwise buff torso. Someone was sitting in the back seat with Andy—someone Connor didn't recognize—when Andy removed his shirt. The unknown man swiped his abs with an alcohol wipe and jabbed him with a syringe. Andy tensed and sucked in his breath as the plunger forced the golden liquid in the syringe into his flesh. A single drop of blood appeared on his skin as the needle was withdrawn, and Andy's face tightened in pain. He tried to breathe evenly. He didn't notice the butterfly that was perched on the car door. It gently opened and closed its wings before fluttering away.

Jax caressed the face of the woman next to him as they lay together in bed. She was a beautiful woman—older than Jax—who looked young, radiant, and happy. Connor understood that they had just made love, and felt intrusive, but in this strange dream state he couldn't really come and go as he wished. He was just a spectator into the lives of his friends. He saw Jax wrap his arms around the woman and pull her close to him, breathing in her scent and closing his eyes—a man glowing and satisfied. Connor saw that Jax wanted to someday marry this woman; she was the love of his life. Suddenly, Connor's heart filled with despair. He wondered if he, himself, would ever find such a soulmate.

Simone and her mother knelt before a small table that was covered with a silk scarf and made into a little altar. A statue of the Virgin Mary knelt in silent piety with a crucifix in the middle of the table, surrounded by flickering blue candles. Connor had the sense that Simone and her mother had been kneeling there for a very long time, and Simone's knees were aching. Connor had been inside Simone's house before but had never seen this altar. Simone's mother's eyes glittered with intensity. She whispered fiercely to her daughter, "Again! Again!"

Simone's lips moved in an inaudible murmur as she recited a prayer over and over. "Hail, Mary, full of grace…" The rosary beads slipped through her fingers. Her eyes were glazed and far away. Connor saw that this was a secret and frequent ritual, and that Simone hated it. Simone saw it as punishment, for what she didn't know, and her mother saw it as salvation; as long as she made Simone do this, her daughter would remain healthy. She would never spiral back down into the abyss of seizures which had nearly consumed her.

Karen was in the upstairs bathroom in her mother's house, vomiting into the toilet. Finally, she stood up, rinsed her mouth out with water from the tap, and stared into the mirror. Her face was sallow and pale. Sweat pasted a few stray curls down to her temples. A single tear escaped her right eye and rolled down her cheek. She dashed it away angrily, as if her body had betrayed her. She looked terrified, confused, and alone.

Connor awoke from his dream and grimaced at the stiffness in his neck and back. He glanced at his cell phone's clock: 2:35 A.M. He was cold and exhausted. He took a deep breath and realized he could not fathom spending the rest of the night in this armpit of the city. He stumbled to his feet and made his way out into the night. He was glad that the rain had let up a little. It was still drizzling, and his wet hair chilled him to the bone. *How do people like Izrael Hands live like this? Not knowing where your next meal is coming from...no warm and dry place to sleep...no bed with real sheets on it...no computer...no microwave...no magic refrigerator with its endless supply of food...no family...no friends...* The enormity of Connor's loss began to weigh him down. Each step forward became an effort.

An hour later, he dragged himself up the front steps of a porch to a small house in the suburbs. He hesitated before ringing the door bell. Completely exhausted, he reached out and pressed the button, wincing as the loud chimes seemed to make the house vibrate.

He rang it a second time, and finally he heard movement on the other side of the door. He saw a light turn on from an upstairs window. Connor had only been to the high school guidance counselor's house once before. He hoped this wouldn't be too awkward.

"Who is it?" the guidance counselor's voice called out from the other side of the locked door.

"It's me, Mr. Salazar. I'm sorry to wake you up, but I need a place to stay," Connor said. He tried his hardest not to cry.

DAY FORTY-THREE

"Peter, I'll be back around eleven. But as far as Mom is concerned, I was back at eight-thirty, right? *Right?*" Karen quizzed her younger brother. Making deals with a thirteen-year-old was always an iffy prospect at best. Karen and Peter's mother was out of town for the weekend, and Karen was left in charge. Peter's cooperation was best secured with suitable bribes. "The pizza's coming in half an hour, and there's money on the hall table, 'Kay?" No response. "*Okay?*"

Peter slouched his way in from the kitchen, eating a banana. "I got it, I got it," he said, waving his hand in the air. "Just go."

Karen grabbed her purse and car keys. She had already dropped her mother off at the airport. The car was hers for the weekend. "And *please* try not to destroy the house, all right?" She was going to see her father for the evening, and Peter was glum about this, as usual. He couldn't visit his own father, who was locked up in prison for molesting Karen, his stepdaughter, two years previously. Peter still didn't have a very clear idea of what had happened and why, only that *something* had happened with Karen—something that made his mother divorce his dad and send him to jail.

Peter waited until his sister was out the front door. He paused and listened for the car engine to start up. Then he turned around and headed for the back door, tossing the banana peel into the kitchen trash on the way. "Got it. The pizza's coming. Make sure we destroy the house. Oh yeah, and Snake-Eye is on his way!" he said aloud, as if reciting a checklist his sister had left for him. He laughed to himself.

Peter opened the back door and smiled. There stood three of his friends who had been waiting for him.

"Well?" he asked them. He put one hand on his hip.

"Well, *what,* you nimrod? We're here for class. We're ready to learn!" answered Flynn.

"Is your sister gone yet?" a sandy-haired boy with freckles and glasses asked anxiously.

"Yes," Peter said. "Do you guys have the goods?" He continued to block the doorway.

The three boys suddenly looked furtive, glancing around to see if anyone was watching. The third boy, a chunky redhead of nearly fourteen years, reached into his back pocket. He pulled out something pink and lacy.

"Not here! Put that away, Tony! You want the whole world to see?" Peter hissed. Tony quickly stuffed the object back into his pocket.

"Well, are you gonna let us in, or what?" Flynn asked impatiently.

Peter stood aside and motioned with his head to enter. "And five bucks each for Snake-Eye?"

"Yeah, we have it. We have everything, Peter," replied Roger, the kid with the glasses.

The pizzas arrived before Snake-Eye did. He was late for everything—all the better for making grand entrances.

"Hello, ladies. Am I late for your little tea party?" Snake-Eye asked as he sauntered into the living room. The boys looked up from stuffing their faces with pizza, and Peter jumped to his feet.

"Hey, Snake-Eye. Great! You made it. We're all here," he said. His face was anxious. Snake-Eye Pelosino was two years older than the rest of them, having been held back two grades. His dad was in state prison, and Snake-Eye, himself, was rumored to have done time at a juvenile detention center. He rolled his own cigarettes and annoyed the teachers at school by calling them by their first names.

Snake-Eye removed his backpack and sat down on the ottoman in the living room. He started to unzip the pack and then looked up, making eye contact with every one of his rapt pupils. Then he simply held out an open palm and waited no more than two seconds. It was instantly filled with three five-dollar bills.

They all turned to watch Tony as he struggled with a handful of change and several crumpled bills that he extracted from his pocket. Three rumpled ones were deposited with the five-dollar bills, but one kept falling on the floor. Tony grunted as he picked it up, twice, and then counted out change into Snake-Eye's palm. The other boys were dead quiet as he did all of this; only the sounds of their breathing and the clinking of coins landing into Snake-Eye's hand were audible.

"There," Tony whispered, finally finished. "That's all of it. Five bucks, right? You said five bucks?" Snake-Eye merely looked at him. Tony looked uncomfortable. "You can count it. I swear it's all there!"

Snake-Eye merely stared Tony down, and then closed his hand around the money, depositing it inside the backpack. Then he slowly pulled a dark-colored bottle out of its depths. "Ladies, I've brought my good friend, Jack, for our little class tonight," he announced, holding up the bottle for the boys to see. Their eyes grew wide. "Meet my buddy, Jack Daniels."

The bottle was passed around and added to the paper cups of Coke the boys were having with their pizza. Peter went to the pantry in the kitchen and came back with two six-packs of beer. He would have to figure out how to replace them before his mom came back Sunday night. Cans popped and fizzed as Snake-Eye began the class.

"Now, ladies," he began, pulling a lacy white bra out of his backpack. "We're gonna learn how to unhook these babies. Front closure, back closure, two-handed and, my personal favorite, the one-handed technique. We'll need a volunteer, but before that, did everyone bring something for show-and-tell?" Everyone snickered.

The boys all anxiously looked at each other. Tony proudly pulled the lacy pink thing out of his back pocket again. He held it up for all to see.

"A thong. Victoria's Secret," Snake-Eye remarked appraisingly. "Very good, Tony."

Flynn produced a black lacy bra, stolen from his mother's dresser. Peter tossed another white bra onto the pile. He also added a box of tampons, which elicited a flurry of nervous giggles from the audience.

"Well, well, well. It looks like Peter's going for extra credit tonight, ladies," Snake-Eye grinned. "And remember, there *is* going to be a quiz!" He turned to Roger. "Annabelle? Do you have something to share?"

Roger's face reddened. He fidgeted for a moment, staring at the floor. Then he opened a paper bag and withdrew a red rubber bladder with a long tube attached. A white plastic tip was at the end of it. "I couldn't get any underwear," he mumbled. "But I found this in the back of the closet. I don't know what it is."

The rest of the boys erupted into laughter. Peter punched him in the chest. Tony pegged an empty paper cup at him. Only it wasn't quite empty, and Coke splattered onto Roger's shirt and onto the beige carpet.

"Whoa, Roger!" Peter cried. He was rolling on the floor in fits of giggles.

"Roger, you idiot!" Flynn exclaimed.

Roger tried to shrink back behind his glasses. "What? What is it?" he asked Snake-Eye, bewildered.

"Class, class!" shouted Snake-Eye over the commotion. "Can anyone here share with young Roger what this thing is? Anybody? Anybody?"

Peter raised his hand from where he had rolled on the floor. "I know! I know! It's a *douche bag!*" This brought more guffaws and laughter from the peanut gallery. Flynn threw an empty beer can at Roger's head but missed.

Roger hung his head and then looked up again, his face a mask of misery. "What's a douche bag?" he asked Snake-Eye.

Snake-Eye picked up the bizarre contraption and held it up theatrically. "This, ladies and gentlemen, is a vagina-cleaner."

Suddenly, the room grew silent as the boys stared at the contraption in awe. Somehow a vagina-cleaner now rated higher than the few bits of lace and elastic the other boys had managed to scrounge up. They couldn't tear their eyes away as Snake-Eye lectured on its use. Roger puffed out his skinny chest a little.

"You fill this part with water and vinegar," Snake-Eye said, pointing out the large rubber bladder. "And this part—" he wielded the elongated plastic nozzle—"goes up you-know-where."

The boys were fascinated and amazed. How did he *know* all this stuff? Secretly, they each wished they'd brought something that goes up you-know-where. Well, there were the tampons, but those were fairly pedestrian; they were everywhere. But this thing, this was a *device*—one of those secret feminine things that belonged to some other mysterious world. They were paying Snake-Eye for a sneak preview of this world.

"So, any volunteers? We're gonna need a volunteer to demonstrate this thing!" Snake-Eye announced. The room erupted into chaos again. Beer cans went flying. The pizza boxes were knocked to the carpet, scattering crusts, crumbs, and tomato sauce everywhere. Flynn started dancing on the couch, pretending to do a striptease. Peter ran upstairs to Karen's bedroom to see if he could find anything to top Roger's contribution. Tony grabbed Roger in a headlock to give him noogies. Snake-Eye simply took another long gulp of Jack Daniels out of the bottle and smiled admiringly at his class.

Moments later, Peter appeared in the doorway of the living room. "Hey guys, check *this* out!"

He was wearing the red jacket. He knew Karen had hung it in her closet. There was a pause in the pandemonium, and then cheers and toasts arose. "Hey, man! That's cool! Where'd ya get it? Lemme wear it!" they all cried out in unison.

"All right, class! Simmer down!" Snake-Eye called out. "Let's get to work!" He picked up the black bra from the pile.

§§§§§

The sound of breaking glass brought Jax out of a light sleep. He looked at the clock, ten minutes after midnight. He'd only been asleep for half an hour or so. He fumbled for his cell phone on the table next to his bed, and flipped it open.

"Hey, Boogerhead," he mumbled into the phone.

"*Jax,*" Karen blurted.

Jax sat up quickly. She sounded like she was crying. "What's the matter? Are you okay?"

"Not really," Karen sniffled into the phone. "But that's not why I called. I kind of need some help over here. Can you come over?"

"I'll be right there!" Jax said. He flipped the phone shut and pulled on his sweatpants and a t-shirt. He was getting good at slipping in and out of the house quietly.

He found Karen in the driveway of her house, pacing back and forth. Her face was streaked with tears.

"Hey, you," he said softly as he approached. When he reached her, he wrapped his arms around her. "What's the matter?"

Karen shook her head. "You have to come inside and see for yourself. My mother is going to *kill* me, that is, after I kill Peter."

She led Jax in through the front door of her house and they stood in the doorway to the living room. Jax stared in open-mouthed horror at the scene. "*Ohmigod,*" he said. He couldn't think of anything else to say.

The house looked as if a horde of Huns had charged through, horses and all. Lampshades and knick-knacks were broken and scattered all over the floor; pizza boxes were upside-down on the carpet; beer was soaking into the couch cushions; an empty bottle of Jack Daniels was on its side in the hallway; and wet tampons were stuck to the ceiling. Two boys were sprawled on the floor. A third boy was puking into a house plant. More commotion was coming from the kitchen. Jax and Karen looked at each other wide-eyed and ventured inside.

"*Hey,* big sister!" Peter opened his arms expansively. He still had the red jacket on. "Welcome *home!* Want some panka—packa—want some pancakes?" He waved a spatula at her, dripping pancake batter down the side of the stove. A black lacy bra had been lopsidedly strapped to his bare chest. Two eggs had been dropped on the floor what looked like quite some time ago; it would take a sandblaster to remove the goo from the ceramic tiles.

Karen recognized Tony Spaulding, the redhead kid from down the street, standing in front of the open freezer. "Hey, I found the ice cream scoop!" he shouted, pulling a metal scoop from where it had become embedded in the ice cream. Butter pecan ice cream stuck to it as he pulled it out. Excited, he stuck the scoop in his mouth.

His eyes flew open wide as he immediately tried to pull it back out. The frozen metal scoop had stuck to his tongue, and he quickly yanked it out of his mouth. "Agh!" he cried in a panic. Blood started oozing down his chin.

"*Ohmigod! Ohmigod! Ohmigod!*" Karen cried, taking in the multiple disasters everywhere. What was she going to do with a half-dozen drunken boys who had already destroyed most of the house?

Jax assessed the situation as best as he could and launched into action. He grabbed a kitchen towel and ran it under cold water. "Here," he said to Tony, stuffing it into his bleeding mouth. "Suck on this and don't move."

Karen went to close the still-open freezer door, and pulled out a pair of pink lacy panties from inside. "Ohmigod, whose are *these?*" she exclaimed.

Suddenly, an ear-piercing shriek made her drop the panties on the floor. She clapped her hands to her ears and wished for this to all go away. *Now what?*

The pancakes in the frying pan had burned and started to smoke, setting off the fire alarm. Jax awkwardly stood on a chair to reach up and disconnect it. He climbed back down and stood in front of Peter, yanking the dripping spatula out of his hand. "Where do these kids live?" he demanded. "We have to get them all home *now.*"

"Nooo! No, no, no!" Peter wailed, shaking his head too hard. He lost his balance and began to sway dizzily back and forth. "We're having a seep—a slip—a *sweep*over after class! And we haven't had our quiz yet! There's a quiz!"

Jax grabbed Peter by the shoulders and made him stand still. "Do their parents know they're here? That they're spending the night?"

Peter nodded vigorously, making himself sway again. "Of course they know! They know what a *sweep*over is, fer cryin' out loud!" He began to giggle uncontrollably.

Jax looked at Karen and sighed. "Well, I guess we can take them all home tomorrow. At least then they'll be hungover—not drunk. Let's get them all herded into the basement, shall we?" He grabbed Tony and Peter by the backs of their necks and propelled them into the hallway. Peter was still giggling; Tony just moaned as he held the bloody towel to his sore mouth. Jax managed to get them all down the basement stairs without killing anyone. As he closed the door, he remembered when he and Karen and their friends used to have sleepovers down there in the finished basement. They'd engage in hard-core pillow fights, have marathon video sessions, and overindulge in way too much pizza and soda, but they'd never had a drunken binge at the age of thirteen.

In the living room, Jax rolled over a body on the floor and recognized Scott "Snake-Eye" Pelosino. Jax scowled at the punk and hauled him to his feet. This kid was bad news; Jax didn't have a doubt in his mind that Snake-Eye was the source of all of this mess.

"*You! Out!*" Jax shouted. He propelled Snake-Eye to the front door, letting him stop only to pick up his backpack, and slammed the door behind him. He watched through the side windows to make sure the kid was leaving, and heard him muttering as he left. At least he looked able to walk.

Once Jax had gotten the two other boys down the stairs to the basement, he threw some pillows and a couple of old comforters at them. He knew where they were kept in the downstairs closet; he had been there so many times.

He found Karen scraping egg yolk off the floor in the kitchen. "I'm too afraid to go back in the living room," she told him with a stricken look. "This was horrible. I shouldn't have left him alone."

Jax turned and went back into the living room to assess the damage. He sighed. Cleaning up the whole mess was going to take *hours*. He slowly walked into the kitchen again and watched Karen work on the stovetop for a few moments, which was covered with drippings of pancake batter, before he spoke. "Um, Karen?"

She whipped around, unsure what to expect this time. She had seen it all tonight. "I'm afraid of what you're going to say next," she muttered.

"Does your mom have any, ah…extra wallpaper hanging around?" Jax winced.

Karen stared at him in shock. She leaned back against the counter, a sponge in one hand and a dishrag in the other, and closed her eyes. "I can't believe I left him *alone*. I can never leave the house again!"

§§§§§§

Peter awoke with a splitting headache in the early hours of the morning. He looked over to see his friends sleeping on heaps of blankets and sleeping bags on the floor. They looked like a litter of big puppies passed out after playing too hard. He stumbled into the bathroom to pee, and once back in the basement he paused in front of an old dresser. Carefully sliding the top drawer open, he reached underneath the clothes and junk to find the framed photograph he kept there.

It was a picture of him and his dad. Peter was just nine years old at the time, and they had gone on a camping trip—just the two of them. They had spent the whole weekend at a lake, fishing and hiking and staying in a cabin; roasting wieners and marshmallows over a fire; getting muddy and dirty and telling knock-knock jokes. It had been the best weekend of Peter's young life. In the picture, he and his dad were smiling at the camera. They were squinting in the bright sunlight, standing on the dock with their fishing poles in their hands. Now, at thirteen, Peter understood that something rare and valuable had been lost and would never come again. Even once his dad got out of prison, things would never be the same.

His eyes stung as he stared at the picture: the two of them looking as if they hadn't a care in the world, as if nothing could touch that golden day. He hugged the picture to his chest, still wearing the red jacket, and smiled. In spite of his hangover, he had a sudden clear vision.

He was visiting his dad, who was old before his time, and Peter was a man himself. He had grown up without his father, and their relationship had struggled along as a series of sporadic visits. His dad lived in a one-room flat that had a microwave and a hot plate, but he hardly used them. These days, he mostly just drank. His eyes were bloodshot, his hands shaky, and his skin had an unhealthy puffy pallor. Peter felt pity and contempt struggling with the love and hero-worship he'd felt as a boy. He knew his father's life had been reduced to drinking his way through each day and night. Peter, himself, felt strong and vital and alive in a way his father had never been. His father, in this snapshot of the future at age fifty-eight, was simply waiting to die.

Peter put the picture back inside the dresser drawer, face down, in its usual place. The vision disappeared, but the memory of it was quiet and powerful and stayed with him. With his head still pounding, he collapsed back onto his sleeping bag and rolled himself up in the red jacket, making a promise to himself to never become a drunk like his dad.

§ § § § §

Jax sprawled out on the living room couch, exhausted. Karen, equally exhausted, was nestled into his side. "Ugh. What time is it?" he whispered.

"Five-twenty," she mumbled back at him. The night sky was beginning to get light. But the house was still standing; the kitchen was clean, with every surface scraped and washed; the living room was decent, with the carpet and cushions cleaned up and a small patch of wall covered over in spare wallpaper. Only one lamp had been broken beyond repair. Overall, the two of them did a pretty good job fixing and hiding all of the damage.

Karen sat up suddenly. "Hey, that little pinhead still has the red jacket on, doesn't he? I can't believe I didn't yank that thing off of him! He better not have puked on it!" she warned.

"Mmm hmmm," Jax moaned. His eyes were closed.

"Did you hear me?" Karen tapped him on the arm. "We should go downstairs and—" she broke off, sat up sharply, and got up and dashed into the bathroom.

Jax sat up on the couch, surprised to hear Karen vomiting. She didn't drink any of the beer that had been scattered all over the house. A few minutes later she came back to the couch, looking pale and ill.

"Are you okay?" he asked her, feeling awake now. "Are you sick?"

Karen slumped back down on the couch and held her head in her hands. "Jax," she whispered hoarsely. "I've missed a period. I'm sick all the time. I think I'm pregnant."

DAY FORTY-NINE

"Are you ready for this?" Simone whispered to Celeste. The two girls stood on the front step of Connor's house. Celeste wore the red jacket, which looked oversized on her small frame. She had folded the ends of the sleeves back so they didn't cover her hands.

"Do you think that's his dad's car?" Celeste asked her, pointing. She glanced nervously at the Pontiac sitting in the driveway. "I think we should come back later if his dad is home."

"Connor said his dad is never home at this time of day," replied Simone. "Let's just do it." She rang the doorbell while Celeste looked on anxiously.

"What if Connor's mom calls the police on us?" Celeste asked quietly.

Simone rolled her eyes. "Shush! She can't call the police on us; we haven't done anything!" she hissed.

Celeste nervously glanced over her shoulder. Simone glared at her. "Will you *relax?*" she said with exasperation. She shook her head and waited. *Celeste seems jumpy as a cat these days.*

Finally, the door opened and Janice stood before them. Her face was puffy and free of makeup.

"Hi, Mrs. Mack," Celeste said quickly. She smiled politely and pointed at Simone. "Um, this is my friend, Simone."

Janice nodded. "Come in, girls," she said softly. She stood back to let them enter and didn't seem at all surprised to see them. They followed her into the living room and sat down on the couch. Connor's mother perched herself on the edge of her favorite lounge chair. She stared at the floor for a long time.

Celeste and Simone glanced at each other, wondering if they should say something. Neither girl knew what to say.

Janice sensed their uneasiness and sighed. "I suppose you've come for his things," she said.

"Yes," Simone answered, and both girls breathed a sigh of relief. They had been afraid of causing some kind of a scene. They weren't sure how Connor's mother would react to them being there and hoped they'd be able to just pick up his stuff and leave as soon as possible.

Janice nodded and stood up. She began to pace the living room floor. "Do you know that Connor was born right here in this very room?" she asked them. Surprised, both girls shook their heads.

Janice smiled a rueful smile, devoid of joy. "Yes, he arrived a little early," she said, placing her hand to her chest. Her eyes had a faraway look to them. "He was a beautiful baby—and a beautiful young man."

Celeste and Simone glanced at each other and instantly shared the same confused thought. *It's obvious that she misses him! Why didn't she stand up for him when he came out to them? Why doesn't she search for him now?*

Janice turned to the two girls sitting on the couch and stared at them. Her expression was worried, beseeching. "You have to understand that John—Connor's father—had such high hopes for him. He always wanted him to follow in his footsteps and become an attorney. His ultimate dream was to have him someday become a partner at his law firm," she explained.

The girls nodded politely. They didn't speak.

Janice continued. "You can't imagine how proud John was when Connor was born. But they never—" she hesitated to find the right words. "They just never seemed to make a connection. You know?" She implored the two girls for understanding, as if she needed for them to be on her side. "John tried to get Connor interested in softball, and he never wanted to do it. He tried to be a good father by taking him hunting and fishing when he could. But it was tough for him with his busy schedule, you know?"

The girls nodded in unison again.

"He always had a lot of responsibilities at the firm. He became even busier when he was promoted to DA, but he *always* made time for Connor. Or at least he tried. Connor just didn't respond though," Janice said with a shrug. "He hated fishing and hunting. That was really tough for John; he had gone to these same places with his *own* father. To him, it felt like Connor was rejecting him. You have to understand how hard that is for a father—how unfair."

Celeste was too afraid to show emotion or speak. She looked awkwardly over at Simone. Simone took a deep breath. "Did anyone ever ask Connor what *he* wanted to do?" she asked. Celeste's eyes widened, but she was relieved that Simone was sticking up for their friend.

Janice looked taken aback. She thought for a moment. "Well, he just wanted to draw pictures, and read, and play violin. Those aren't really things you can do together as father and son," she said in a slightly defensive tone.

Celeste began to feel enraged. She cleared her throat. "Mrs. Mack, may we please pick up Connor's things?" she asked, trying to remain calm. She was already uncomfortable, and now it felt as if she were betraying Connor, listening to his mother defend his father.

Janice stared at her then slowly shook her head. "I'd say yes, but it's all gone. John cleaned out his room and got rid of everything," she said, ashamed. Her voice fell to a whisper. "I tried to stop him—to talk to him. He wouldn't listen."

Celeste stood up, furious. "Everything? Even his artwork? His *sketchbooks?*"

Janice raised her voice. She was not going to have a young girl making her feel worse than she already did. "You have to understand that this has been incredibly difficult for John!" she pleaded.

"Well, it's no picnic for Connor either!" Simone cried. She stood to leave. "Come on, Celeste. I think it's time to go." Celeste nodded. Her cheeks felt hot. The two girls headed toward the front door.

"Celeste—" Janice followed after them. "Please!" Celeste stopped and turned around, waiting. "Please tell me where my son is."

Celeste and Simone exchanged hesitant glances. Celeste hated being put in the middle of things, but Connor was her friend and she owed it to him to do what she could to keep him safe. "I'm sorry, Mrs. Mack. He asked us not to tell you," she replied. Celeste had been coming over to the Mack's house since she was eleven years old, and while she had never felt overly welcomed, Connor's mother had at least been courteous toward her. She suddenly felt guilty. "But he's okay," she added quickly. "He's taking care of himself."

Janice nodded, suddenly choked up and unable to speak. Impulsively, she stepped forward and clasped Celeste in a fierce hug. "Thank you," she whispered. Celeste gasped. It wasn't because the hug was so tight that it made her unable to breathe, but because she suddenly had a vision.

Her husband is cheating on her, and her son is gone. She's alone and trapped here, in a prison of her own making, and she's too afraid to rock the boat—to do anything. She has depended on other people taking care of her for so long that the thought of changing anything scares her to death. She doesn't know how to do anything on her own. She doesn't speak up for herself…like her son does.

Celeste stepped back, surprised. *What is going on? Why did I just see that? This is none of my business!* But she saw everything with the same clarity she'd experienced earlier, when she'd seen Connor's parents shouting at him, angry and disbelieving. It was as if she had been standing in the room with him. Now she had a flood of unwanted images about this woman, about her sad and confined life, and she had to get away.

"Goodbye, Mrs. Mack," she said, and hurried out the door. Simone followed close behind her.

§ § § § § §

Jax glanced around the clinic waiting room and took in the bright, happy-looking paintings on the walls. *They're making an effort. I can't imagine anyone being very happy here, but at least they're trying.* He was the only male in the room, sitting next to Karen, and he wondered if people thought he was the father. There were about a dozen girls and women waiting—some with friends and some alone. One girl had an older woman with her, who appeared to be her mother, and no one smiled. Well-worn magazines lay inert in laps, except for a few who studied their contents with the concentration of a brain surgeon. Everyone in the room, at one time or another, slipped a glance at Jax and Karen.

Jax folded his hands carefully in his lap, studiously not touching Karen. He wanted to be here for her, but he didn't want to give people the wrong impression. They probably already had the wrong impression, and were trying to decide whether he was a decent guy for coming in with her, or a scumbag for knocking her up. *We're just friends, all right? I didn't do anything. What does it really matter what any of these people think anyway?*

Karen's eyes were red and puffy. He wondered if she had slept at all since they'd gone to the drugstore together to get an over-the-counter pregnancy test.

Positive. It had been positive. *It could be wrong,* he'd told her. *These things aren't all that accurate, you know.* Karen had shaken her head. *I have morning sickness. I've missed a period. My breasts are tender. I'm pregnant.* Jax had felt a surge of pure rage then, anger at the callous way what's-his-name at that stupid party had used her and left her. Then his anger had spilled over onto Karen. *What were you thinking? Why did you drink so much? Why didn't you make him use a condom?* Karen had just cried, and shaken her head. *I was drunk. I didn't know what he was doing. I didn't know what I was doing...*

Now Jax felt bad that he'd given her a hard time. She was obviously suffering and had a big decision to make. But he had his own issues weighing heavily on his mind. His heart pounding, he had signed in at the clinic's front desk and asked for an examination, too, without saying anything to Karen.

"Jaxon Montclair?" a uniformed nurse called out. Karen looked at him in surprise.

"I'll, um, be back in a minute," he said to her. He quickly stood up and followed the nurse through the doors to an exam room.

Minutes later, he was sitting on a paper-covered exam table—naked from the waist down—and wearing a paper gown. It seemed like forever until the doctor came in to see him. His heart sank to see that she was a woman. *Please, couldn't it have been a man? But I suppose this is a women's health clinic. What did I expect?*

"I have these, um, sores that I need to have checked out," he mumbled to the female doctor. His throat was dry as he spoke. He closed his eyes and waited for the grim diagnosis.

§§§§§§

Simone and Celeste accidentally knocked on the wrong door. "Connor's out back," the man who had answered the door told them. "It's the room attached to the garage." They couldn't call Connor since he'd gotten rid of his cell phone; he'd said he couldn't afford it anymore. There were a lot of things he couldn't afford anymore, but at least Mr. Salazar had found him a place that wasn't too expensive. He also graciously dug up some clothes for him and provided him with a pair of sneakers, a wool sweater, and a toothbrush.

Connor was glad to see his two friends, but his face betrayed his bitter disappointment when he saw that they only brought one brown paper bag between the two of them.

"Nothing?" he asked them incredulously.

Both girls shook their heads. "Sorry, Connor. We tried..." Celeste muttered. She flung her arms around him. Distracted, Connor disentangled himself and sat down on the bed—a mattress on the floor and a threadbare old duvet. He gave a mirthless chuckle. "So, my father got rid of *everything?* Even my art books?"

Simone nodded. She set the large paper bag on the floor and pulled out a new sketch book and a flat tin box of drawing pencils. "But Celeste and I stopped by the art store downtown and got you these," she smiled earnestly. She held the materials out to Connor. "It's not much, but maybe it can help with starting over?"

Connor just stared at the gifts as if they were poisonous snakes. A great wave of rage and helplessness threatened to suffocate him. *What the hell? I've just lost my entire life and this is supposed to replace it? There were years of drawings and paintings in those books! Everything that meant something to me has been destroyed—probably thrown in with the garbage and dog shit—and this stuff is supposed to make me feel better?* His face turned red and he clenched his fists.

Celeste took the drawing tablet and the pencils from Simone and knelt down on the mattress next to Connor. "Connor?" she asked, holding the gifts in front of him. "Connor's artwork *then* might be lost, but Connor *now* is probably an even *better* artist," she said, trying to diffuse his anger.

He looked into her sweet brown eyes and saw fear and apprehension. His heart contracted, as if a great fist had punched him. *What am I thinking? Isn't this exactly what Izrael Hands was warning about? I am so concerned about my earthly possessions that I almost insulted my friends. I even got angry at their gift! He was right. I need to cut all my material ties to my old life because they only drag me back into the past and make me feel bad. But Izrael had to have been wrong about friends. How could I possibly cut them loose, too? They are all I have and I would never abandon them the way my own parents abandoned me...*

"Thank you," he said in a choked voice, taking the tablet and tin box from Celeste. He set them carefully on the floor next to the bed, and wrapped one arm around Celeste. "Thank you both," he said, reaching for Simone's hand. Tears flooded his eyes. Simone knelt down on his other side and he enveloped both of them in an embrace, holding on as if he would never let them go. "Thank you, my friends," he whispered over and over. The three of them sat together, dissolving into a mass of tears.

Finally, Simone pulled away and grabbed the paper bag. "Oh! Look! We brought you groceries." She reached in and pulled everything out to show him. "Blue corn chips!"

"Those have more fiber than the regular ones," Celeste informed him matter-of-factly.

"I guess the blue ones are irregular, eh?" Connor grinned. It took a second for Celeste to understand what he meant but she punched him on the arm as soon as she did. "Ow!" he cried, rubbing his arm.

Simone pulled out more items. "Canned tuna, whole wheat bread, mustard, bean dip, apples, raisin boxes, and your favorite…Lucky Charms," she announced.

Celeste looked around the small, dingy room. "This is quite a place, Connor."

"It's two hundred dollars a month. I have my own bathroom. Mr. Salazar helped me find it," Connor explained. "He knows the guy who owns this house."

Simone got up and went to look inside the tiny bathroom. "And water? Does it come with running water? Or do you have to pay extra to flush the toilet?" she joked.

"It has water!" Connor laughed. He grabbed the bag of blue corn chips and tore it open. "Where's that bean dip?"

Celeste found it underneath the box of Lucky Charms and opened the can for everyone to share. They each took a scoop with a blue corn chip and held their chips up.

"To friends," said Connor.

"To the future," exclaimed Celeste.

"To regularity and running water!" added Simone.

Connor broke out into laughter. It was the first time he had truly enjoyed himself in a very long while.

§ § § § §

Jax and Karen sat in the car in the clinic parking lot. Now that they were alone, Jax felt comfortable holding Karen's hand.

"When's your appointment?" Jax asked her.

"Next Tuesday at 1:00 P.M. I'm going to have to skip school," Karen replied. "They said I'll probably be up and able to go back on Wednesday. Will you come with me?"

Jax nodded. He turned and looked at her frankly. "Do you need money?"

She hesitated. "Well, it's going to cost $550. I have $470 in my savings account. I'll have to ask my mom for the rest. Don't worry though. I'll come up with something good."

"You're not going to tell her?" Jax wondered.

"Are you *kidding?* The one who burst into tears when her son sprained his wrist? Who forgot to renew her driver's license, didn't know there was a bench warrant out for her arrest, and spent a night in jail? My mom doesn't need anymore trouble, *trust* me," Karen said, rolling her eyes.

"Don't ask her for the money. I have it. I have $200 in my closet," Jax offered.

Tears suddenly filled Karen's eyes. "Thank you, Jax. I'll pay you back, I promise." She knew he was saving for an electric guitar. This was a generous offer.

The two of them were quiet for a few minutes. Finally, Jax spoke. "Karen, are you sure you want to do this? You don't have to, you know."

"I know, Jax," Karen said with a half smile. "When I have a child, it's going to come into this world wanted and planned. I want to be ready. There are just too many unwanted babies here already to add one more."

"There's adoption…." Jax's voice trailed off.

"I know. I've thought about that. I've been thinking about it ever since I started thinking I was pregnant. But there are already babies and children here who need homes—some older children and some with special needs. It's irresponsible of me to add one more. It was irresponsible of me to conceive this baby in the first place."

Jax was silent for a moment. "This is your *child*, Karen. Are you really sure about this?"

Karen bowed her head and a sob caught in her throat. "I know, Jax, I know. And I love this child enough to *not* want to bring it into the mess that is my life. My own mother had me when she was young—too young to be a mother—and Peter and I have had to muddle along in spite of it. Two fathers have left us; you know how the second one went," she said softly. She wished that Jax would drop the subject altogether.

"Yeah, I know," Jax mumbled.

Karen continued. "Well, what if this child had to go through all that? Even if the adoptive parents seemed okay, there are no guarantees. Jerry seemed like a decent guy when my mother married him, but then he turned into a child molester! I can't protect this child, Jax. I can't stand the thought of it possibly growing up the way I had to. I will bring a child into the world when I have a real life, when I can raise it and protect it," she said firmly. She leaned back in the passenger seat and closed her eyes, exhausted.

"Okay," Jax responded, nodding. "I guess I'm not the one who should be talking about being responsible." His shoulders tensed and he let his breath out slowly.

"What do you mean?" Karen asked, slightly confused. She had found it a bit strange that he had set up an appointment to see one of the doctors but figured it was just to get condoms or something.

"The doctor thinks I have herpes," he blurted.

"*What?*" Karen opened her eyes and stared at him. "Are you serious?"

Jax looked straight ahead, studying the license plate of the car parked in front of them. "And they took blood for an HIV test," he added.

"Jax. I'm—I'm so sorry. HIV? Really? Do you think...?" Karen cried.

"Anything's possible. I'll get the test results in three days," he sighed heavily. "Whatever happens, I'm going to have to go talk to Jasmine." When he turned to look directly at Karen, his face was full of pain. "She's the only woman I've ever been with."

And she's not worthy of you! Karen wanted to scream. *Look at what she's done to you! What are you doing with such a lowlife?* But she couldn't give a voice to her thoughts. She was in the condition she was in by consorting with a lowlife, too.

Again, the car was silent. "I'll come back here with you when you get your results," Karen said firmly. "Everything will be okay."

DAY FIFTY-TWO

"Well, who knew the history of litigation in the Roman Empire would be so *interesting?*" Simone grinned at Andy, who lay on the floor surrounded by notes, papers, and a couple of library books. They were working on a term paper in his bedroom. The door was open; it was a requirement of Andy's mother.

"Just shoot me now," Andy moaned. He closed his eyes. "Why did I wait to work on this until the day before it's due?"

"You always leave it until the day before," Simone reminded him. "Why ruin a perfect record?" She scrolled through the notes Andy had written on his desktop computer to see what he had come up with so far. "Dude, you can't just use Internet sources. You'll get a C, for sure. You have to have *real* sources—you know, like, from reference books."

Andy picked up a sheet of notepaper and placed it over his face, as if to hide from the term paper. "*Dude,*" he said, imitating his girlfriend. "What's the matter with Internet sources? Wikipedia's a real source!"

"It's lazy. English teachers see right through it. It's not thorough, and you need to reference everything in the bibliography," Simone explained. She sighed and started typing, her gaze intent on the screen.

Andy pursed his lips and blew out a little puff of air, experimentally raising the paper up from his face and letting it settle back down. Deciding he was enjoying this, he tried it again. "What's the matter with a C? A C is a passing grade," he said.

Simone stopped what she was doing and turned around. "Andy, a C is *average*. None of the good colleges will even *notice* a C on a transcript," she chided him.

Puff. The paper poofed out again and settled back on his face. "Simone, I'm not going to get into college because of my transcript.

I'll be getting in on a football scholarship." He *had* to get in on football; his grades just weren't good enough otherwise.

In fact, football was his only chance and he knew it. Most of his free time was spent on the track, in football practice, and in the gym—another reason why his English paper had been left until the day before.

He felt Simone kneel down on the rug next to him. She lifted the paper off his face and kissed him on his mole. "And what if…? What if you do all this training to get into college football and the day before tryouts, you wreck your knee? Or you're in a car accident and break a leg? Or you get some weird blood disease that doesn't kill you but makes it so you can't play football?" she asked. "Anything can happen, Andy. You need to be prepared academically."

Andy rolled his eyes. They'd had this conversation before. "I'm not gonna wreck my knee. Simone, I'm not smart like you. I'm never gonna get by on brains and good grades. Football is what I do," he said.

"Even with football, you still need to keep your grades up or you'll lose your scholarship," Simone quipped. "You know that. And Princeton has a great learning center for people with dyslexia. Yale does, too."

Andy raised himself up onto one elbow. "Princeton, huh? Yale? You've already checked this all out?"

Simone glanced down at the floor, and then back at his face. Her expression was bright and hopeful. "Well, sure I have. It doesn't hurt to plan ahead, does it? They both have great microbiology departments, too," she said dreamily.

Microbiology was going to be Simone's major when she got to college. It was incomprehensible to Andy. She went on in a rush of excitement. "You have to live on-campus for the first year—they're all like that—but after that, well, there's plenty of off-campus housing and apartments. There are some great gyms in downtown New Haven, Connecticut, and we wouldn't even need a car. The bus systems run all the time, and—" She fell silent, realizing that Andy was watching her with an expression she had never seen before. He looked so *guarded,* so closed-off.

"And…?" he asked, his eyes cool. "And what if I decide to go to the West Coast? What if I can't get into an Ivy League school? If you went to Yale, would you fly out to California during spring break to visit your dumb football player boyfriend?"

"What?" Simone asked, shocked. "What are you talking about? Andy, you're not dumb! I never said you were dumb! I just mentioned about the learning centers, because, you know, I thought it would help your situation." Fear gripped her heart. *Did I offend him?*

She knew there was nothing wrong with being dyslexic. It was just a condition like anything else—like having asthma, or bad eyesight, or crooked teeth. *Or seizures.* She knew that people with conditions simply did what needed to be done to overcome them. She smiled apologetically and cuddled up to Andy on the floor. She tried to hug him, flinging one arm across his chest. *There's that odd sensation again—something with his chest. It's not hard and muscular as it used to be. But he still looks big. I don't get it. Are his pecs more...prominent and soft?*

Andy sensed Simone's brief hesitation after she hugged him. Scowling, he turned away from her and crossed his arms over his chest. Doggedly, Simone slid her arms around his waist and tried to hug him close. All she wanted to do was get *through* to him. She wanted him to understand how much she loved him. More importantly, she wanted him to stop this ridiculous thinking about being dumb. "It's going to be all right, Andy," she reassured him. "We'll be together wherever you end up. It doesn't matter to me. I can go to school anywhere."

Andy held his breath, wishing this moment would go away. *But I can't,* he thought darkly to himself. *Football is the only thing I have. If I can't get a scholarship, I'm sunk.* Ever since having his sights beyond college football, he promised himself that he would do anything to be competitive and have a successful career. While he was used to telling Simone everything, he knew she might not understand the lengths to which he was prepared to go. He wondered if she was catching on that something was different about him. He hadn't thought that the side effects of steroids would be so...noticeable. *There's no stopping now though.*

Restless and agitated, Andy sat up and shook himself free of Simone. "I'm hungry," he announced. This was no great surprise to her. He was always hungry. "Let's go out for Chinese. I'll finish this stupid paper later."

§§§§§§

The knot of tension in the pit of Jax's stomach threatened to expand and take over his entire body. He and Karen were back in the clinic, and he was getting the results of his HIV test. At the moment, he could no longer form a coherent thought in his head. He wished he could trade places with Karen; at least she knew what her problem was, and what was going to be done about it. If he were HIV positive, there would be no getting over it. HIV at sixteen? Of course, there were drug treatments and all of that, but at this moment it was all too huge for him to get his mind around. He silently prayed that the situation wouldn't escalate that far.

Karen had to have blood drawn for tests before her procedure on Tuesday, and she waited with Jax in the lobby. Since he was too distracted for conversation, she had started talking to a thirteen-year-old who was there by herself. The girl was obviously frightened, but was trying to cover it up with a false bravado. She looked so young; she barely had breasts. *What complications of the adult world landed her in the women's health clinic?* Jax wondered. He watched, wordlessly, as Karen smiled at the girl and talked with her.

The girl's name was Cindy. She was skinny and had mousy brown hair tied back in a ponytail. Her eyes nervously darted around the room and she startled like a frightened rabbit every time one of the nurses came into the waiting room to call a patient. "I hate needles!" Cindy declared to Karen. "I'm not having any needles! They're not gonna get any blood from me!"

"It's not so bad," Karen said softly. "It's just a little prick and then it's over."

Cindy folded her arms across her chest in defiance and continued her rant. "They said they had to do some tests, but they're not getting blood from me!" she vowed. "I'm not letting any needles anywhere near me!"

The girl's voice was drowned out by the tidal wave roaring in Jax's head. He couldn't keep the endless loops of doom out of his head. *If I'm positive, how would I be able to keep it from my parents? If I'm positive, then Jasmine infected me. I just can't believe it. Not her, not Jasmine. She's the love of my life; I'm sure of it. How would I tell her? How would we deal with it? How will I ever get married and have a family someday?* He had already envisioned Jasmine and himself with two children, all traveling together on concert tours. *My dreams could be over any minute now. Please, God, please help me...*

Karen stood up. "It's my turn," she said to Jax, touching his shoulder. "I'm going in to get blood drawn." She picked up her bag and turned to Cindy. "You can come and watch if you want. I don't mind."

Still defiant, still declaring that no needles would touch her skin, the girl agreed to watch the procedure. She got up and crept after Karen, staying close. Out of curiosity, Jax followed them both into the small lab, too.

Cindy crouched by the doorway, still muttering, while the technician applied a tourniquet and wiped Karen's arm with a swab. Karen turned to Jax and started chatting with him about school, about his family, and about playing in the band. She looked directly at him as she talked; he knew she was trying not to look at the needles and tubes. Soon, her face grew pale and tension formed around her mouth. Jax simply nodded and said "yes" and "uh huh" periodically, unable to focus on what she was saying for more than a millisecond.

"Okay, that's it," said the technician. She unwrapped the tourniquet from Karen's arm.

Karen feigned surprise and looked at the discreet bandage on the inside of her elbow. "That's it? You're done? You're kidding. I didn't feel a thing!" she lied, smiling at Cindy. Jax wondered if the girl saw the effort in her face.

"Yep, it's pretty easy and painless," the technician said, winking at Cindy.

"Well, this must be one of the most talented blood-drawers this side of the Mississippi. I thought a mosquito had landed on me. C'mon, Cindy. You'll hardly feel a thing," Karen smiled, motioning over to the young girl. To Jax's amazement, the thirteen-year-old allowed herself to be coaxed into the seat.

"Don't you go anywhere!" Cindy exclaimed, grabbing Karen's arm. "You're staying with me, right?"

"Sure, I will," Karen replied. She took hold of Cindy's hand and squeezed gently. Cindy looked around wildly, like a cornered animal. Jax smiled and took her other hand. "See? Jax will stay here, too. He's my best friend. And guess what? He plays the guitar!"

Karen chatted away, trying to keep Cindy's thoughts occupied, while the technician did her job. The girl flinched, but didn't cry out, and Jax felt her small hand tighten around his. *Where are your parents, little girl? Where are your siblings? Does anyone look after you?*

"There you are," another uniformed nurse exclaimed, stopping short in front of the doorway of the lab. "Jaxon Montclair, right? We're ready for you. Come with me, please."

Jax remembered nothing after that—not what he said to Karen or how he got to the doctor's office, or even how he and Karen got home afterwards.

§ § § § § §

At 8:45 P.M., Jax walked up the front steps to Jasmine's apartment. He paused and studied the door, remembering the first time he'd gone inside after sitting in her car for nearly an hour. He had sang for her that night. *She loves my music. She wanted to hear me sing my own music, and then we went inside.* He remembered every moment of that night: the overwhelming hope, desire, and excitement he had felt. He remembered that by the time he finally got home at 4:00 A.M. the next morning, he was head over heels in love. He had never felt like this about anyone before.

"Hey, Jax," Jasmine seemed happy to see him and let him in. They embraced and kissed, but only for a moment, and Jasmine pulled away. She was wearing the tight blue sweater he liked so much; her braids were loose around her shoulders. She was achingly beautiful, and he wanted to hold her and close his eyes and let all of this disappear. Instead, he just stared at her wordlessly, afraid that when he opened his mouth the dream would end. They would never be able to recapture that exquisite beginning, or the magic that had sprung up around the two of them so quickly after that.

"What is it, Jax?" Jasmine asked him, her expression concerned. "I know you. I can tell that something's wrong."

How well you know me! Yes, we do know each other, and our love is strong enough to get through this. We are so in touch with each other that you know instantly when something is wrong. But it's going to be okay. As long as we're together, it's going to be okay...

Jax took her hands, and led her to the bed so that they could sit down. "Jasmine, you know I—" he began. His throat suddenly felt dry. He cleared it and started over. "We care about each other, right?" *That sounded dumb.*

"Well, sure, Jax," she answered him. There was caution in her voice. Her eyes were somehow darker than they had been a moment ago—less open, less inviting.

"There's something I need to tell you," Jax went on, desperately hoping for some other way to say this—something clever and sweet and disarming—but all he could do was tell it as it was. "I have these, uh, sores, and I went to get them checked out."

Jasmine's face took on a guarded, watchful look. "*Sores?*"

"Yeah, you know, um, *sores*," he gestured vaguely below the belt. "Well, I had some tests done, and it turns out that I, uh, I have herpes. And they said you should, you know, you should get checked out, too."

Jasmine stood up and walked the length of the room, which wasn't far. Turning around, she had her hands on her hips and an angry expression on her face. Jax was stunned. This was a face he had never seen before, a Jasmine he hadn't known existed.

"Jax, are you telling me you've given me *herpes?*" she demanded.

"I—I—" he stuttered.

"You know that herpes isn't curable, don't you? You've given me something nasty and incurable. You understand that, *right?*" she hissed. Her eyes were huge, furious.

"No—Jasmine—it's not, I mean, herpes can be controlled. They told me there are things to take to control outbreaks, but—" Jax could hardly find the words. He was suddenly so shattered. A lump formed in his throat. To his horror, he thought he might cry in front of her. He took a deep breath to compose himself. "Jazz, all you need to do is get checked, and, uh—and they said to get a, um, you know, an HIV test."

Fury filled Jasmine's face. Somehow she was no longer beautiful; she now looked like a twenty-four-year-old who was simply trying too hard. "An HIV test!" she screamed. "Are you telling me you've given me AIDS, *too?*" Her eyes darted around the room like she was looking for something to throw.

"No!" Jax cried. "No, I tested negative! I don't have it, but you know, they said, to be on the safe side, since you know, the herpes is there, you should—we should—"

"We should *what?*" Jasmine barked. "No, I know what I *should* have done by now. I *should* have told you about me and Luke!" She looked venomous.

Jax was confused but tried to stay calm. "You and Luke? But you said you had broke up with him…" *This is not happening. Please, can't we just go back? Back to where we were before?*

"We did, but we're getting back together. In fact, I'm moving into his place," she stated. Her expression softened a little; perhaps she did have a heart after all. "I know I should have told you before, but I didn't want to hurt your feelings." But suddenly her eyes hardened again. "*Herpes! Jax, w*hat am I going to tell Luke? I can't believe this!"

A fog of pain filled Jax's entire body, threatening to engulf him and make him incapable of speech. He had to speak now, before that happened. "Jasmine," he choked out. "You were the first one. The only one. I never—I've never been with anyone but you."

There it was, hanging in the space between them. And in Jasmine's hardened crystallized eyes, he saw the truth.

She knew. She's known all along. She never bothered to tell me, and never mentioned using a condom. She told me she was on the pill. She somehow forgot to mention that she has herpes—and maybe something more. Jax shuddered as he recalled the strange vision he had had of her on that first night. She had appeared wasted, gravely ill, and practically unrecognizable.

Jax lurched to his feet and headed out the door as fast as he could. He wouldn't bother to take the bus back home; the long walk was what he needed to clear his aching head and his breaking heart.

DAY FIFTY-SIX

Karen had been able to borrow her mother's car, and she and Jax sat quietly after she shut the engine off. They were sitting outside of Connor's place, late for the birthday party. But somehow neither one of them could be the first to open the door and get out.

Finally, Karen spoke. "You really had no idea that she was still seeing Luke?" she asked.

Jax shook his head. "No, I can't believe it. We seemed so good together. We were so *right* for each other—so in tune, you know?" His voice was quiet and dull as if someone had pulled the plug on him. Karen hated the sound of despair in his voice. The suffering in his eyes was something she'd never known in him. And she hated Jasmine, a woman she had never met, and never wanted to now.

"You're better off without her, Jax!" Anger and bitterness gave Karen's voice a sharp edge. "She gives *you* something, and then tries to put it all on *you?* That's complete BS! How dare she? I mean, you never did anything to hurt her!" A sob caught in her throat. "You know she must've gotten it from Luke, and then gave it to you!"

"I know," Jax said, deflated.

Karen's heart threatened to pound its way out of her chest, full of all the things she wanted to tell him. *Jax, it was all wrong. She was using you to get back at her boyfriend. You were just there at the time. You didn't have to go there. You could've been—you would've been—better off without her. You would've been better off with me! I would never have done such a thing to you.* Self-loathing struggled with outrage and shame inside her. *Who am I to talk though? Look at me now. Look at the condition I'm in. I can't believe what I have to do tomorrow. No one's to blame but myself. It's all my fault. Ohmigod, what stupid mistakes we've made...*

Karen turned her reddened, tear-streaked face to Jax. His eyes widened as he made eye contact with her. "Jax, she didn't deserve you.

You are so much better than that. You deserve someone who will treat you with real respect—someone who *really* loves you." *You are so much better than me. I don't deserve you either, but I want you more than ever. Even when I try to replace you with someone else, it never works. Nothing ever works. Why did I even think anyone else could take your place? Even if you don't love me, I still love you. I always will, too.* Her hands gripped the steering wheel until her knuckles turned white.

"Karen? Are you okay?" Jax's honey-hazel eyes filled with concern. He placed a hand over one of her tightened ones and rubbed it gently. "You don't have to worry about me. I will get over this. I'll get through it."

Karen couldn't speak. She just nodded and gripped the steering wheel even more tightly.

"Are you worried about tomorrow?" he asked gently. "I would be. I can't imagine what you must be going through..." His hand on hers felt like velvet. She breathed a little easier. "I'll be there, you know. I promised you," he added.

And if this were your baby, I wouldn't be doing this, Karen thought. *As if I will ever be in a position to have your baby...* She nodded again and risked a look at him, hoping to see something there that matched her own feelings. Once again, she only saw the face of a truly concerned friend. She peeled her hands from the steering wheel and got out of the car.

§ § § § § §

"Hey, what *took* you guys so long?" Celeste demanded once they were inside Connor's little room. "We already cut the cake! Here, it's strawberry. Simone and Andy made it." She held out a glop of colorful confection on a paper plate, urging Karen and Jax to try it.

Karen took it from her. "With, um, blue frosting?" she asked, hesitating. Jax was relieved to see a small smile on her face.

"Andy got carried away with the food coloring!" Celeste laughed. She turned to Jax. "Here, you need one, too." She handed another paper plate to him.

"It's supposed to look like the *sky*," Andy muttered to no one in particular.

"Yo, happy birthday, Connor," Jax said to Connor, who was lounging on the mattress on the floor. Connor grinned at him. Simone sat cross-legged next to Connor, and Andy was in the only chair. The floor was littered with bags of potato chips, Cheese Doodles, and wrappings from fast food burritos. Jax studied the remains of the birthday cake in its pan on a little table. "So, um, what's this here? An alien?" he joked. A runny squiggle in chocolate icing adorned the remaining half of the homemade cake.

"It's a *condor!*" exclaimed Simone indignantly. She turned to Connor. "Anyone can plainly see it's a *condor!* You know, we used to call you 'Condor' when we were kids?" Connor smiled and looked at the guys in the room as if the girls were crazy. He didn't say anything.

"Told you it looked like road kill," Andy muttered to her. She laughed and socked him in the stomach.

"No, really, it's a fantastic cake," Connor assured Simone. "The best. In fact, I've never seen a more gorgeous cake. Thank you." Simone beamed proudly.

"Oh, PS, Jax won't eat anything that doesn't have dill pickles and chili pepper on it," Karen joked.

Jax glanced at her, pretending to be hurt by her comment. "*Fine,* just this once..." he said with a grin and took a big bite of the cake. Everyone waited for his reaction. "Mmmm, wow! This is the best blue-strawberry condor cake I've ever had in my *life,*" he concluded. Simone punched him in the knee. "Hey! I said I *liked* it!" he cried.

"So, we were playing a game before you guys walked in," Celeste explained to Karen and Jax after everyone said their hellos and had some cake. She pulled Karen down to sit on the floor next to her. Jax made a space among the wrappers and bags and sat down cross-legged next to Andy.

Celeste continued. "Since this is Connor's seventeenth birthday, and he's moved out of his parents' house already, we're trying to guess what we'll all be doing in the next five years—you know, like after college and all that."

"Yeah, and we had just gotten to Celeste," Connor informed them. "I predicted that in five years she will still have that freakin' red jacket on!" he laughed.

Celeste was, indeed, wearing the red jacket; its cuffs were turned up as usual. "Uh huh, please ignore the man on the bed," she teased. "He just wandered in and wasn't invited."

"Hey now! I'm the *birthday boy,* you lunchbox!" Connor cried out in fake disbelief. Everyone broke out into laughter.

"So, Karen, what do you think I'll be doing in the next five years?" Celeste grinned happily. She slipped her arm through one of Karen's arms.

Nothing. Celeste will be doing nothing. She will be staring out a window with a vacant look on her face, tied to her chair with a soft cloth to keep her from sliding off; her body will be lax and inert. Her hands, lying like dead birds fallen into her lap, won't be playing the violin or holding any books. Karen immediately leaned away from her, shaking her head in shock. *What on earth?* She realized everyone was looking at her curiously and froze.

Karen laughed nervously, her face tense. There was no way she could tell Celeste what she *really* thought, or knew. She smiled a fake smile. "Celeste, you will…you are…going to be a cocktail waitress at Club Med. On San Tropez. Or, um…you'll be starting your Master's degree in particle physics—or some other kind of science that I don't understand at all!" she announced.

"Yeah!" said Connor. "That's exactly what I thought, too!"

"Very funny!" replied Celeste. She rolled her eyes playfully and lifted her chin up. "Actually, you'll all be seeing me on the cover of *Vogue*. I'll be famous and everyone will know me as C, thank you very much."

"C?" asked Jax, confused. "Like the letter C, or the ocean 'sea,' or like 'see that condor in the frosting-blue sky?'" He tried to keep a straight face but broke out into laughter again.

"The *letter* C! Like middle C on the piano!" Celeste said, standing up for her future moniker.

"How about you, Karen?" asked Simone. "What are you going to be doing in five years?"

"Ah, she'll probably be married with three kids by then," joked Connor, waving his hand nonchalantly in the air. Jax looked quickly at Karen's face, seeing the fear and shock hastily covered over with polite amusement. He knew she probably wanted to throw up after hearing Connor's comment.

"No, Karen's going to go out and save the world first," Celeste piped up. "All those starving, book-deprived children of Botswana are counting on her!"

Karen stared at the floor for a moment, her eyes glistening, but she quickly recovered. "You know, perhaps it would be a more interesting game if we all took turns wearing the red jacket," she suggested. "Whoever's wearing the jacket can predict the future. We won't even have to guess what will happen in the next five years!"

Connor gave her a surprised look. "What do you mean?" he blurted. His expression took on a guarded, anxious quality. Andy looked up sharply, too. He frowned and suddenly seemed anxious.

Karen hesitated. She looked around the small room at her friends. "Well, has anyone ever, um, had anything weird happen when they were wearing the jacket?" Her heart sped up as the vision of Celeste being senseless and tied in her chair burned in her mind. *Maybe this wouldn't be a good game to play.*

"You mean like an out-of-body experience or something?" Simone asked, giggling. "That might be weird." She glanced at Andy but his eyes wouldn't meet hers.

"Well, I just mean—I don't know," she said with hesitation. She decided to choose her words carefully. "Okay, fine. When I wore the red jacket, I experienced something like a dream—only I wasn't asleep. It was more like a flash of insight—a *preview* or something." Her eyes seemed bright behind her glasses, animated and alive.

Jax's face darkened. He looked at the floor. *I wonder if...?*

"Come on, Karen," Celeste nudged her. "What have you seen? Has something weird happened to you?" She seemed slightly alarmed and was already taking the red jacket off.

Karen shrugged, suddenly unsure whether she should continue. "Not really. I mean, it's just a feeling I sometimes get. Maybe it's nothing," she said with a shrug. Deep down, she knew it was more than nothing.

"Here, put it on," Celeste urged. "Then you can tell us what you see!" She held the jacket up with one hand and waited for Karen to take it from her.

Karen was suddenly shy. She shook her head. "No, not me! Someone else can try it," she said.

"Andy!" Celeste suggested. She sprang up from her position on the floor next to Karen and held the jacket out to him. He immediately shook his head and folded his big arms across his chest.

"Come on, Andy," Simone cajoled. "You know I love this jacket on you." She tried to pull his arms out while Celeste pranced in front of him, holding the jacket up.

Andy shook his head vehemently. "No, it doesn't fit me."

Simone nuzzled his cheek and tried tickling him to get him to uncross his arms.

"It's not always a preview," Connor interjected.

Everyone turn to stare at him. He shrugged, looking a little nervous. "I once met this guy—a homeless man. He touched my arm, when I had the jacket on, you know?" His face was thoughtful as he remembered the encounter. "And then I just *knew* things. I knew his name—or at least what he calls himself these days—and that he was divorced. I knew that he was a drug addict, too. Honestly, it was a little crazy."

Andy grabbed the jacket from Celeste, relieved that the attention was no longer on him. "Okay, *you* put it on then, man!" he said.

"Yeah, tell us what you see," Jax urged. He tried to shake off his unpleasant vision of Jasmine. Like Andy, he was glad that he wasn't the one putting the jacket on at the moment.

Connor grinned, but his eyes looked anxious. He took the jacket and stood up. Slowly, he inserted his arms into the sleeves.

"Wait!" Celeste shrieked excitedly. "We should make it *authentic*—like a séance or something! Turn the lights off!"

Jax reached over and flipped the lights off. Simone carefully lit two candles and placed them on the floor. The flickering candlelight made Connor's face glow. Everyone stared at him, waiting.

"I did see something, or maybe I dreamed it," Connor said. "When I was going home—the day I decided to tell my parents—I had this vision of my father." His voice faltered for a moment, and his brow furrowed with tension. "He was tearing my clothes out of the closet…dumping the drawers out…pulling posters off the wall—all in a complete *rage*. I had never seen him like that before."

He stopped and looked at the rapt faces watching him. "I thought my imagination was just going wild because I was anxious about telling them. But everything I envisioned actually happened—*everything*." He looked over at Simone and Celeste. "And then when you guys went back to get my things, everything was gone. He had gotten rid of it all."

Celeste's eyes were wide as she listened to him. "I saw that. I—I saw it, too," she whispered.

"Before it happened?" Simone asked incredulously.

Celeste nodded. "It was when we were walking out to the parking lot after orchestra practice," she explained, biting her lower lip. "I saw the look on your father's face, he—he was a *maniac!* He was so full of hatred!"

"And you said something at that time," Connor added. He leaned forward, his face tense. "I remember that you suddenly said maybe it wasn't a good idea to talk to my folks. I had thought that was weird because up until then you had always said I *should* tell them."

Celeste nodded. "I—I didn't know it was really going to turn out so badly. I just thought, I don't know, that I was imagining things." Suddenly, a thought occurred to her. "But Connor, when I had that vision of your parents, I wasn't wearing the jacket. You were!"

Karen spoke up. "Were you touching him, C? Did you touch the jacket while he had it on?"

Celeste thought for a moment and then nodded. "I *did* touch him. I touched the sleeve. It was such a strong vision. It had been like I was standing right there. Ohmigod, I wish I had done a better job warning you, Connor! If you hadn't told them, you wouldn't be here now! You'd still be at home!" She looked as if she were about to cry.

"It's okay, C. It doesn't matter," Connor reassured her. "It was going to happen someday, and I told them when I told them. Even *I* didn't think they'd take it so badly." He sounded a lot calmer than he actually felt. There wasn't a day that had gone by since then that his heart didn't seize and shudder as he thought about that scene—the last memory he had of his parents.

Jax spoke up. "I can't believe they'd want to throw you out just because you don't want to go to law school," he commented, shaking his head. "That's so harsh."

"Yeah, my folks wouldn't be too happy if I told them I wanted to be an artist instead of an athlete, but they wouldn't throw me out," added Andy. "I'm sorry, man."

Connor's hazel eyes teared up a little; his face reddened. He looked at his two male friends, slightly confused. "That's not—they didn't—you mean you don't know?" he asked incredulously.

"Know what?" Jax asked, bewildered.

Connor glanced at Celeste. "You didn't tell them?"

Celeste shook her head. "It wasn't my news to tell."

"Mine either," added Simone.

Connor took a deep breath and looked back at the guys. "My parents kicked me out because I'm gay," he announced. "My dad said, and I quote…" Connor fell silent. His voice instantly went dry as his throat constricted involuntarily.

"His dad said he'd rather have a *dead* son than a *gay* son," Celeste finished bitterly. Both Andy and Jax looked uneasily at Connor, their faces guarded.

With shock, Connor realized that they suddenly looked like strangers.

DAY FIFTY-SEVEN

Neither Jax nor Karen could borrow a car during the day, so they took a bus downtown. Jax planned to bring her back home in a taxi, but at least they could save a little money on the way to the clinic. Jax tried his best to keep up a little small talk during the bus ride, but Karen was lost in some other place. Eventually, he fell silent. At every bump and sway of the bus, he could feel her gently leaning against him; he didn't move away. Finally, he wrapped his arm around her shoulders and pulled her closer as if to shield her with his own body. He felt helpless and wished he could do more.

Irrational thoughts crowded his mind as frustration and anger roiled in his gut—*I should have been there. Why didn't I go to that party? If I had been there, this wouldn't have happened. I would have seen that guy coming a mile away and Karen would never have left with him.*

Even though Karen tried to say it hadn't really been rape, Jax was outraged. His right hand clenched into a fist as his left hand grasped Karen's shoulder even tighter. He saw the guy at the party clearly in his mind's eye—*back off, asshole, what do you think you're doing? Get your hands off her. Get away from her!*

He imagined grabbing the guy by the throat and throwing him across the room. In his imaginary replay, Jax kicked the guy as he tried to get back up—the man pleading for Jax to stop—but there was no stopping. Jax punched him in the face and then hauled him to his feet. As soon as the beaten guy was standing, Jax socked him in the gut again and then throw him out the door. A primal surge of satisfaction entered his mind as he imagined the man tumbling down the stairs, begging for mercy. The man's anonymous face suddenly morphed into a familiar one—Karen's stepfather, Jerry. Jax ran down the imaginary stairs and kicked him again. *You don't touch her, you hear me? You don't even look at her! Get out of here and never come back or else!*

Karen felt Jax's arm tighten around her shoulders, and she could feel his tense and rapid breathing. Glancing at his face, she was shocked to see an expression of rage—his brow low and furrowed, his eyes glittering, his mouth a tense line under flared nostrils. She had never seen this Jax before, a man who looked as if he could tear someone apart at that very moment.

Jax, what's the matter? Are you angry with me? I'm sorry! I shouldn't have done it. I was stupid, she apologized in her mind. And yet, for all her worry about Jax's apparent anger with her, she felt oddly safe, as if no harm could ever come to her with his arm around her like that. She liked that he held her steady as the bus leaned and lurched. Tears pricked at her eyes as she thought again of how she had disappointed him—how she had disappointed everyone. *I just want this to be over.* But she didn't want this moment on the bus to be over, sharing a suspended moment with this fierce and angry Jax. She had never felt so safe in her life.

The bus stopped and they needed to get off at their stop. Jax did not let go right away. Instead, he looked deeply into her eyes. She saw something there, a staggering force of emotion—rage, fear, longing, frustration, regret, hope, despair, and uncertainty. Karen felt as if he were looking straight inside her, as if she had no defenses—definitely none of the usual walls and smokescreens she hid behind. Jax's right arm slid up and around to join with the other, completing a tight circle with Karen inside, and he hugged her for a moment, his face against her neck. *I'm so sorry, Karen. I'm so sorry that this has happened. I'm so sorry that I wasn't there when you needed me the most.*

Then he was up and out of the seat, pulling her along behind him. Karen's head reeled as she struggled to hold back her tears.

§ § § § §

"What do you mean, you don't think you're going to college?" Simone demanded. She and Andy were sitting in the front seat of his dad's car, at their favorite spot. A half-empty bottle of vodka rested on the seat between them, which they had been using for spiking their Cokes.

"I didn't *say* that," Andy retorted. "I just think I might need a year off after high school. Like I said before, I don't think I'll make it into some Ivy League school."

This was *not* exactly what Simone had in mind for fun when they first drove out to the water tower. She had been friendly and cuddly when they first parked, and had snuggled up in his lap, kissing him fervently.

But somehow he had been distracted, and finally had pushed her away, making the excuse that he wanted to pour them drinks instead. The alcohol made her feel warm and inviting, but when she tried playing with his shaved head, he moved away uncomfortably. Then he dropped this bombshell.

Simone's mind began to race. *What is he talking about—a year off? No college? Where does that leave me? Where's the 'us' in this? Am I supposed to go off to college without you? We'd be spending a year apart? We need to be together, don't you understand that? How could you even think of anything else?*

"Well, what would you do with a year off?" Simone asked, trying to remain calm. "What's the point of waiting?" She knew that a year apart would just have them spinning their wheels, languishing without each other.

Andy didn't reply. He sipped on his mixed drink and stared blankly through the car windshield.

An impossible thought crossed Simone's mind, filling her with anguish. "Andy, are you seeing someone else?" *I can hardly believe I'm saying this.* To her horror, Andy didn't answer right away. The silence in the car suddenly took on a cold chill. Simone felt her heart constrict. "Andy?" She couldn't help the shrill edge which crept into her voice. *Don't! Please don't say it! This is not happening!*

Andy glanced at her and then away, concentrating on something outside the car window. "I just think…maybe it would be better…if we, you know, started seeing other people," he mumbled.

"What? Seeing other…?" The roaring in Simone's ears made it hard to concentrate. "Andy, I don't want to *see other people!* Andy, this is *you and me.* We have something! We have something together that other people aren't lucky enough to have. We *understand* each other!" She reached for his hand, but when she took it there was no response, no sweet embrace of his big warm hand around hers.

Finally, he looked back at her shining eyes, her anxious face. "No, Simone, I don't think you do," he said coldly. The words hit Simone with a physical impact.

Her eyes pleaded with someone who had already made up his mind. *Can you not feel this? Don't you know what you're doing to me? Please stop this!*

But he went on. "I'm not smart like you, Simone. I'm good at football, but the rest of it—all the college stuff, all the academics—I've never even liked it. I can't compete with all you brainy people," he said.

"No, Andy, don't say that! You don't have to compete with me at all. I can help you, I *want* to help you!" Simone begged.

"I don't want you to *help* me," Andy replied. "I just think we need...some space." He slowly withdrew his hand from hers.

"Space?" Simone cried, her voice edgy. "*Space?* That's what guys all say when they're seeing someone else. That's it, isn't it? It's not about college or any of that. You're already seeing someone else, and you're only just now getting around to telling me!"

The silence in the car was immediate and overwhelming. In fact, it was claustrophobic. Simone needed to get out, to get away, to climb out of this abyss. She grabbed the bottle of vodka and jumped out of the car, ignoring Andy's calls for her to come back.

"Simone, let me at least drive you home!" he shouted.

But she disappeared into the woods without another word.

§ § § § §

Jax waited in the lobby for hours, restlessly leafing through old magazines, and discovered that he really didn't care who was looking at him and what they might be thinking. He wondered what had happened with the girl who had been here last time, what was her name? Sandy? No, Cindy. She had been so frightened, so anxious, and Karen had worked her magic on her. *Karen has always been good like that.*

Remembering that day at the clinic, how nervous he, himself, had been and what a wreck that poor girl had been, and how Karen had calmed them both, Jax pulled a scrap of paper from his backpack and began to write. This was a song of emotion, of hope, of the connections people all have with each other and how people need each other. Memories of Jasmine, never far below the surface, surged up and held him mesmerized with a paradoxical mixture of pleasure and pain: the unbearable sweetness of her love; her amazing smile and body; the raw pain of her rejection; and the terrible hollow emptiness of her absence.

High and low. Soaring and crashing. Pleasure and pain. Why is it that life has to include its opposite in everything? Do we have to experience agony in order to feel ecstasy? Jasmine filled his head, his heart, his whole body; he could not stop her from taking him over. The sound of her voice, her hands on his skin, the glow of her sienna-brown eyes—it all held him in thrall. The intense pleasure of their intimate connection had warred with the despair of his last meeting with her. *What is love if it's not shared equally by both, if its golden brilliance can be held in one hand and crushed? Real love, absolute and unshakable love, should be there. It should stand up and make itself known. It should rise above petty concerns and illusions, shining through the rain and making all right again.*

Jax decided that "Illusions of Love" was a good name for a song. *It has two meanings: The illusion of thinking we're in love, and the illusion that love can somehow be crushed or disappear. Its real strength is underneath, making you strong and whole in spite of everything. That's it—love is stronger than all of this. It's stronger than ex-boyfriends; it's stronger than a viral infection; it's stronger than people who become uncertain and confused. Real love is what leads us out of despair. And you know what? I'm going to go tell her that. I can't give Jasmine up without a fight. I can't just let her slip away. I have to go talk to her. I have to show her that we are bigger than this, that our love is deep and real. It will carry us through our problems. It has to...*

Jax wondered how he could have walked out the door so quickly—how he thought he could just walk out of her life. He would go back. He would go see her again and make her understand that in the greater scheme of things they were *meant* to be together. He was certain that the two of them could get through this.

"Mr. Montclair?" a voice called out. Startled, Jax looked up to see a nurse standing in the doorway of the lobby with her arm around Karen. "Karen is ready to go home now."

Jax stuffed his paper and pen inside his backpack and hurried over to meet his friend. Karen's face was pale. Tiny beads of moisture formed on her upper lip, and she didn't seem able to stand up straight. She awkwardly hunched her shoulders and contracted her entire body into itself.

"How do you feel?" he asked her, linking his arm through hers and guiding her across the lobby.

"Crappy," she whispered. Her face was tense and drawn with pain. She walked very slowly, as if balancing a cup of water on her head—water she was terrified to spill. Jax helped her down the front steps and into a taxi, where she leaned on him in the backseat, exhausted.

Karen could feel every little bump and pothole as the taxi sped through the streets. She felt empty and drained, and emotionally raw, but something else was pulsing through her—something warm and unsettling and threatening to unbalance her. Finally, she turned her head to look at Jax. She clutched his hand.

"Jax," she said with quiet intensity. The tone of her voice instantly alarmed him.

"What is it? Is something wrong? Are you okay?" he asked. His heart quickened.

She took a deep breath. "Jax, I should have told you this a long time ago, but I will tell you now—I love you. I love you with all my heart; I always have. I don't ever want to be with anyone else," she said matter-of-factly. "I think that you and I are soulmates, Jax."

He was stunned. *What on earth...? Where did this come from?* "But—I thought—I mean, what about that guy, David?" Jax managed to squeak out. *This is crazy! Karen, what are you talking about?*

Karen shook her head impatiently. "That was nothing. I was just trying to find a substitute—someone else to love because I didn't think you loved me." She turned to him and gasped in pain, having moved too quickly. "But I think you do. We love each other, Jax." Her eyes were moist and shining. Her bottom lip was trembling. Her breath was coming in shallow gasps.

"Karen, I—I don't know what to say," Jax stammered. He was floored. *How can I not hurt her feelings? I have to, but now? When she's like this? Ohmigod!* Jax squeezed her hand gently and tried to smile. He had to be honest with her. "Karen, I'm going back to Jasmine. I have to talk to her, to make her see...I have to..." he said slowly. His voice trailed off. He was unable to sort through the sudden tornado in his head.

Karen's eyes widened as Jax's words stung her; they were pins and she was the cushion. *Huh? Why? What is he talking about? That bitch? The one who slept with her ex behind his back, gave him a nasty disease, and then said she was moving in with her ex again? Is he insane?*

The worst part was the look on Jax's face. It was the look of a concerned, if somewhat shocked, friend. *A concerned friend. No, that's not it! That's not you! How dare you have that look on your face when you're my soulmate! How can you not see it?*

They rode in chilled silence until they got home. Jax paid the taxi driver and then helped her to the front door of her house, where she shrugged him off. "I can manage," she told him breezily.

Jax hesitated, consumed with discomfort. "Are you sure? I can come over later, you know, to check on you," he offered.

"Don't bother," she quipped. The door closed in his face.

§ § § § § §

The vodka was all gone an hour-and-a-half later. It could have been an hour; it could have been three. Somewhere along the way, Simone had lost track of time. She dropped the bottle when it was empty and kept walking, or stumbling, through the woods and then into the subdivisions. Her face was red and puffy, and she didn't think it was humanly possible to cry any more tears. It was late and very cold outside, but the red jacket hung down to her knuckles. She wrapped her arms around herself; at least the red jacket was warmer than a ski jacket.

We were going to live together in Boston. Or New Haven. We were going to have fun in the dorms for the first year—sneaking into each other's rooms, using secret signals for our roommates to leave us alone, going to parties and football games. I would cheer for Andy as he went on to win game after game. Then we were going to get an apartment downtown—our own place with a double-bed, a crock pot, and an ugly coffee table that we'd pick up at a garage sale and even take it with us to our first house. After we both graduated from college, I was going to get my Master's degree and Andy would continue his career as a professional football star. I'm supposed to be the mother of his children someday—beautiful tow-headed kids, with Andy's clear green eyes and no seizures. This was not supposed to happen. How could this happen?

"Miss, are you all right?" a male voice asked, jolting her to her fuzzy reality. A man in a brown coat was standing in front of Simone. She hadn't realized she was wandering all over the sidewalk in this well-populated part of the city. Her hair was a mess and her eyes were red and swollen. Mascara streaked down her face.

"I'm fine," she answered, trying not to slur her words. She was more drunk than she thought. *Where's that vodka bottle anyway?*

The man was not convinced. "May I call someone for you? Your parents?" He was already pulling a cell phone out of his pocket. "Maybe someone can come and pick you up? It's pretty cold out here, you know."

Simone backed away. A horrified image flooded her mind of her mother going completely ballistic. "No! No, I'm f—I'm *fine,*" she stressed and kept walking. Calling her mother? What a disaster *that* would be. If it were up to her mother, she'd keep Simone locked away in her bedroom forever. Her mother hovered over every sniffle, every headache, every ache and pain Simone ever had, terrified that her daughter would wind up hospitalized again with seizures. Simone had become an accomplished actress, always pretending to be in perfect health. Her acting skills had naturally extended to her whereabouts, her comings and goings, and exactly what kind of relationship she had with Andy.

She smoked and drank in defiance behind her parents' backs. *See? I am normal. I can do anything any other girl can do.* Cigarettes and alcohol paradoxically warred with her overachieving alter-ego—the dark shadows behind the star cheerleader, the straight-A student, the biology whiz. She was the bright student who would attend Harvard, or Yale, and get a Master's degree in microbiology. Andy, her perfect, all-American boyfriend—and future fiancé—would pound the turf and bring his team roaring to victory, again and again. She had thought about getting a Ph.D., but that would take too much time away from their family. She planned to be finished with her Master's degree by age twenty-four and get pregnant at age twenty-five. She'd be a cool young mom who would bring the kids to their father's football games. She had it all mapped out.

Except Andy wasn't here. Simone thought he was dumping her, for someone else—but for whom? It had to be what's-her-name—that chick, the one with the red hair, the one who would never speak to her. *C'mon, Andy. I am so much better than that girl!*

Simone decided that she would just have to talk some sense into her boyfriend. If she just explained everything clearly, of course he would see that he'd been blind. He was just having a momentary lapse; he would come around. Their whole future together was too important to throw away on something this ridiculous. Simone *loved* Andy with all her heart. Her love would triumph; it would overshadow everything else.

I just have to find him and talk to him—now. Tonight. Simone glanced over her shoulder and saw that she had outdistanced the man in the brown coat. She looked forward again and continued to make a heroic effort to walk normally. Her head was pounding and her stomach was queasy, but she ignored both of them as best as she could. Her determination to go find Andy and win him back would keep her going strong. Luckily, she knew him well enough to know where he went whenever he got upset: Will's house. *I know he lives somewhere around here,* she thought. *Andy must be at his apartment telling Will what a mistake he made to let me go.*

She continued walking and looking up at the various street signs around her. Finally, she came upon Baker Street. *That's it! That's where Will lives.* She and Andy had been there a few times, and he and Will often watched football on his old TV together. She didn't know Will very well, but she figured Andy might've gone there after she'd left him at the water tower. She tried to hurry on unsteady feet. *Which house is it? A brown house, near the corner, I think...*

She saw the brown house on the corner, and sure enough, Andy's car was in the driveway. *Yes! This is it! This means something. It means we're supposed to be together! It's a sign! I just have to remind him of this. That's why I'm here. That's why I came all this way and didn't even know this was where I was heading. I just needed some time to think things out. I'm fine now. We'll be fine soon. Ugh! Andy, where are you? I'm here now. Things will be okay. I know they will be. You'll see...*

As she approached the house, her nerves started to get the best of her. She reached into one of the pockets of the red jacket for her lighter and her crumpled pack of emergency cigarettes. Shaking, she pulled one from its packaging and lit it. The long drag calmed her down a little. She smiled to herself and dropped the almost-whole cigarette on the ground, crushing it with her shoe. *I'll get him back. I just know I will...*

Simone stepped up onto the rickety wooden porch of the brown house and reached out to steady herself; her feet seemed to forget how to navigate three little steps. From the top of the porch, she could peer through the large central window into the living room. She noticed a threadbare couch against the wall. She also saw the top of Andy's head. Immediately, she was drawn to the scene inside as a moth to firelight.

Yes, Andy was in there. And he wasn't alone. In fact, he didn't have his clothes on—and neither did his female companion.

A gasp of shock escaped Simone's throat as she lost her balance from craning her neck and standing on her tiptoes. She suddenly fell backwards with a loud *thud.* She had seen a pair of lacy underwear next to the couch where Andy and his new friend were; tears of dark rage filled her eyes. It was the worst thing she could have seen at that moment—especially since she and Andy had been planning to save themselves for each other.

But rage was overcome by a sense of horror as a sudden vision came to light. Simone was all alone, weeping in a confined space. Her hair was cut short—but not by her own will—and the knowledge of something awful weighed her down like a thousand pounds of dread upon her shoulders. The guilt came from something far more horrible than Andy leaving her, and in this desolate place she knew she would never see her love again. But she was so drunk that the thoughts simply swirled around inside her, unable to make any real sense or order. If they had, she might not have done what she did next.

DAY FIFTY-SEVEN

Sirens woke Connor from a restless sleep. He was huddled on his mattress on the floor, trying to keep warm. The bluish glow from the digital clock on the floor showed it was only 2:14 A.M. Irritation flashed through him; it would take forever to get back to sleep and he had to be on the bus to school by 6:45 A.M. Now that he no longer lived at home, his commute to school took much longer. On top of that, he had to pay for a student bus pass. Whenever he suddenly awoke in the middle of the night, he could never fall back to sleep. He'd spend the rest of the hours stressing out about all the things he had to do and all the bills he had to pay. His part-time job stocking grocery shelves was hardly enough for everything.

He rolled over and closed his eyes, but the sirens kept wailing. Soon, he heard voices outside. He stretched and decided to check out the scene. Padding to the window, he pulled open the drapes and looked out. His landlord, Chuck, who lived in the main house, was out there with a neighbor. He couldn't hear what they were talking about, but it was clear from their body language that something was wrong. They were full of tension and anxiety, gesticulating and looking toward the east.

Connor clumsily put his clothes on, tied his shoes, and grabbed an old gray sweatshirt. He hesitated a moment. *Where's the red jacket? Oh yeah, Simone has it. Man, she's been wearing it a lot lately. Whatever happened to our sign-out system?* Connor let out a huge yawn and sauntered outside to see what all the commotion was about.

"Hey, Chuck," Connor said to his landlord. "What's up?" It was colder than he'd realized; he could see his breath in the night air. But there was something else, something pungent and invasive in the air—smoke?

"There's a house on fire a few blocks away," said Chuck excitedly. "There are fire engines and police cars everywhere."

"That's awful! Whose house is it? Anyone we know?" Connor wondered.

Chuck's neighbor spoke up. "We don't know whose it is yet, but my cousin lives over in that direction," he said. "We're going to go over and see in a little bit."

Connor knew he would never get back to sleep now, so he walked with the two men five blocks over to where all the action was taking place. The smell of smoke grew stronger and stronger. His eyes were watering like crazy as they turned the corner onto Baker Street.

Connor was shocked to see the whole house ablaze. It didn't look real even though he'd seen such things a hundred times on the news and in movies. But actually being there—feeling the heat from the raging flames; hearing the fire roar like a charging battalion fighting the firemen's hoses—stunned him into open-mouthed silence.

He heard Chuck and his neighbor say that the house didn't end up belonging to anyone they knew, but the chaos of the fire trucks, people shouting, police yelling at bystanders to stay back, and the relentless power of the flames drowned out the rest of their conversation.

Several ambulances, with their lights still flashing, were parked at random angles in the street. Emergency technicians were loading people onto stretchers into two of the rigs. Each fire hose was wrestled by several firemen as they unleashed thousands of gallons of high-pressure water into the flames. It looked as if the white-hot flames were simply consuming the powerful jets of water along with everything else.

A commotion erupted near two parked police cars, and Connor pushed his way through the crowd to see what was happening. Four cops were manhandling a shouting and thrashing young man with a shaved head who was throwing the policemen back and forth. They all collapsed into a writhing mass on the pavement.

Connor couldn't believe his eyes. *Ohmigod! What the...?* He tried to push his way to the front of the crowd.

"Stay back, son. It's under control," warned a police officer in front of him. He held his arms out as a barrier. "You don't want to get any closer!"

"But I *know* him! That's my friend! Andy! Andy! It's me, Connor!" Connor's voice rose in desperation, as if he could make everything right once Andy recognized him. "Andy!"

"Stay back!" the cop shouted in his face. "I mean it! Stay back!" Connor tried to dart forward—he had to get Andy's attention—but the officer grabbed his arm and held him still. "You don't listen very well, kid," he growled.

Andy's reddened face was pinned down against the pavement; he didn't look like he recognized anyone. His eyes were stark and staring, and his mouth was open in a savage bellow of rage that erupted a spray of blood. He still struggled and fought the four police officers who were pinning him down. He was wearing only a pair of navy blue sweatpants. His hands were cuffed behind his back, and the cops were trying to get his ankles together to cuff them as well. Andy continued to writhe and kick and buck with tremendous power.

All Connor could do was stare at his friend's terrifying face, made even more surreal by the red and blue flashing lights on his skin. The heat from the burning house made him feel like he had a pervasive fever.

The conversation between the police officer still holding his arm and another one nearby penetrated Connor's fog of shock and heat and spinning colors and flames. At first, he thought they were talking to him.

"That kid's stacking if ever I saw it," said the officer who was holding him down. "Totally psycho. He's strong as a bull, but wait until they turn him over. He has titties like a girl! It's all the hormones and painkillers and uppers and downers and who knows what else they're mixing in these days. They stack all that crap with the steroids and it does a complete number on kids like him. That kid will be lucky if he can tie his own shoes by the time he goes through detox."

"His name is Andy Greentree," Connor interjected. "He goes to my school. I know that guy!" The two officers stopped talking and looked at him. The one holding his arm finally let go. He pulled out a pad and pen from his shirt pocket.

"All right, kid, come with me," he said in a serious tone. Connor obeyed and followed him to one of the patrol cars. He gave the officer Andy's name and his parents' names, but didn't know any phone numbers or his home address—just that he lived somewhere on the South Side. He did remember Simone's number, so he offered that to the officer.

"Where are you taking him?" Connor asked when the officer was finished with his questioning.

"County Hospital. He's got smoke inhalation, and then they'll probably transfer him to the psych ward," the officer replied.

The psych ward? County Hospital? How on earth did all of this happen? Connor found his landlord again and asked to borrow his cell phone. Simone didn't pick up, so he left her a voicemail: "Simone, it's Connor. Meet me at County Hospital when you get this message. It's an emergency. Andy's been in a fire, and he's…ah, he seems to be having some problems. I'll either be waiting at the emergency room or at the psych ward, but please come as soon as you get this."

§ § § § § §

Celeste happened to glance at the clock on the wall, and was surprised to see that it read 2:14 A.M. Thank God her mother thought she was spending the night at Beth's, where Beth and three other friends were having a sleepover and studying for a history midterm. Sort of. They *might* have had a history book there somewhere…

Celeste was out with Tranh, who had picked her up at Beth's place at 11:00 P.M. It was only an hour-and-fifteen-minute drive from his school, so he'd been coming into town almost every weekend to take Celeste out partying with his friends. Sometimes he picked her up at her home, but they were careful not to do this too often and made a point of coming back at 9:30 P.M.—a rule set by Celeste's parents. She was only supposed to be going out once a week, but the 'study party' at Beth's had provided a good opportunity to meet up, and Tranh was on the road as soon as she'd called him.

He was amazing. He was cool, fun, and sophisticated, and Celeste had completely surprised herself by liking him. In fact, she liked him a whole lot more than she ever thought she would, and she had decided that this was the man she would give herself to—not anytime soon, of course, but *someday*. They had spent a considerable amount of time kissing in the front seat of his car before coming inside, and now they were hanging out with Tranh's friend, known only as Sailor, where he had brought her on their very first date.

"Sailor, man!" Tranh called out as they sat on the floor of the living room. "We need a refill!" Tranh held up two glasses with melting ice in both of them.

Sailor was a skinny redhead guy, and Celeste still wasn't sure how Tranh knew him. He was older—about thirty years old—and he wasn't in school. There were five or six other friends there, and Celeste was having a hard time remembering their names since she had already had several drinks, and something else. *What did Tranh give me?* Celeste giggled, trying to remember. *The sweet smoke? A couple of little white capsules and a mixed drink to wash it down? No, that was last time. Was it? Well, whenever, whatever. All I know is that I'm feeling just fine.*

She began to focus her jittery energy on trying to figure out the name of one particular girl whom she had chatted with briefly when she and Tranh first walked in. *Marney! That was it. The girl with the brown hair and, unfortunately, rough complexion. Yes, her name is Marney.*

Her mother's voice entered her head. *Don't stare at her, Celeste. Remember that Nguyens are never rude people.*

Celeste rolled her eyes. Anyone watching her may have wondered what was irritating her. *Ugh. Seriously, Mom? I don't want to be rude, but may I have a little privacy? May I just have a little time with my friends, and with Tranh?* She smiled as she thought of Tranh in a way her mother would definitely disapprove of, imagining him naked, but then cringed as her mother's voice intruded and immediately harangued her in a shrilly tone that made Celeste sit up a little straighter.

You are a bad girl, Celeste!

Her grandma's voice chimed in. *You're a bad girl! The police will come and get you! The police will take you away. You have shamed your family!*

"Sailor!" Celeste called out. Tranh looked at her in surprise. "Sailor! Where's our refills?"

"Whoa, red alert! Celeste needs her drink!" Tranh laughed. Celeste grinned and stared at him. He really had the most beautiful eyes, and she willed the voices in her head to shut up as she deliberately imagined him naked again.

Another drink appeared in her hand. Tranh's face was swimming in front of hers. "Here, cutie pie. Look what I've got for you. Open up…"

Celeste swallowed the prettiest little pills—a rainbow of the most amazing colors—and washed them down with the drink, which made her cough and gasp. But already a feeling a warmth was overtaking her. It was an intense fire with flames of every color—colors she hadn't even known existed. There were no more voices as the roar of the rainbow flames drowned them all out, even the voice of Tranh.

§ § § § §

Jax's cell phone woke him and he glanced at the clock-radio next to his bed. 2:14 A.M. The phone displayed BOOGERHEAD, and Jax breathed a sigh of relief. He had not spoken to Karen since dropping her off at home, and he'd already left her three messages. No answer until now. Maybe she was still mad at him—exactly *why* was still a mystery to him—or maybe she was just sleeping so much that she simply hadn't had a chance to call him back.

"Hey, Karen," he said into the phone with a yawn.

"It's me, Peter. I'm using her phone," Karen's younger brother said.

Jax sat up instantly, jolted fully awake by the young, frightened voice.

"Peter? What's the matter?" he asked.

"Karen, she's—something's wrong with her. She can't walk. Her face is a funny color," he said in a panicked tone. Jax heard Peter sniffle. "I don't know what to do!"

Jax's heart started pounding. *Something wrong? What on earth? It was supposed to be a simple procedure!* Struggling with himself, he knew he had to remain calm for Peter's sake. "Where's your mom? You need to tell her that Karen is sick," Jax said authoritatively.

"My mom's out. I don't know when she'll be back," Peter replied.

Jax closed his eyes, not sure if this was good news or not. "All right, stay right there. I'm coming over," he said as he snapped his phone shut. He pulled on his jeans and sneakers and scrounged up a long-sleeved shirt and fleece jacket. Stepping quietly past his parents' bedroom, he paused for a moment, wondering if he should awaken them. *What if Karen is really sick? I'll need a car to get her to a hospital.* While he had occasionally slipped in and out of the house without his parents' knowledge, he had never taken a car without permission.

Well, he would get to that once he saw Karen. Maybe Peter was overreacting. *Damn their mom for being out! Where the heck is she?* Jax didn't have time to point fingers. He had to calm himself as he slipped out the side door and walked over to Karen and Peter's house. *Shelley doesn't know; Karen hasn't told her anything. Karen probably just told her mom that she had a cold. She probably said she'd be fine and to just go ahead and go to whatever party she was going to. She probably just said she was going to get some extra sleep. But what if she doesn't wake up?*

Peter had not been exaggerating. Jax was shocked to find Karen collapsed in the upstairs hallway outside the bathroom. Her skin was cold and clammy; her breathing was ragged.

"Karen? *Karen?*" Jax sank down on his knees next to her and gently slid his hand under her neck. He carefully lifted her head up, and saw that there was vomit on her chin and the front of her flannel nightgown. He helped her to a sitting position and leaned her against the wall.

"Karen! Jax is here to help!" Peter cried. "Wake up!"

"Karen? What's the matter?" Jax asked. He stared anxiously into her face. His heart constricted as he realized she hardly recognized him.

"Jax?" she asked slowly. She simply gazed past him, her eyes glassy and blank.

Jax glanced down and saw to his horror that the bottom of her nightgown was stained with blood. "Peter! Go in the bathroom and get some towels." He could hear the boy sobbing as he ran into the bathroom.

Jax pulled his cell phone out of his pocket and snapped it open. His eyes filling with tears, he could hardly see to punch in the numbers, *nine-one-one*. An operator was on the phone in an instant.

"Hello, operator? I need an ambulance," Jax cried. "Please hurry!"

DAY FIFTY-EIGHT

No matter how he tried to reposition himself, the edge of the molded plastic chair in the emergency room lobby pressed into Connor's back in the most uncomfortable places. He was too tall for most chairs, and his head and neck drooped as he tried to prop his chin on his hand. Somehow, he had managed to doze off for a few hours. It was now almost 7:00 A.M. though, and he was going to be late for school. He still hadn't yet been allowed to see Andy.

A woman's shrill voice drew Connor's attention and he turned his aching neck to look down a hallway. A heavy woman with permed hair who was wearing a blue coat was arguing with a young man—a young man who looked a lot like Jax. Connor leaned forward for a better look, rubbing and stretching his neck, and discovered that it was, in fact, Jax. He got up and approached Jax and the woman. She was obviously very upset.

"And you never even bothered! You never bothered to tell me; you never bothered to tell your own parents; you just dumped her off and left her to bleed to death! How could you? How *could* you, Jax? You've known Karen your whole life. She adores you," the woman screamed. "She *trusted* you!"

"Shelley, I—" Jax tried to interject. Karen's mother cut him off.

"This is what comes of taking strangers into your home!" she hissed at him. "I don't know what possessed your parents to adopt strays like you and your brothers, but I never said anything because I knew they couldn't have children of their own. And now look what happened!" The woman's voice rose in hysteria. "Now my Karen's sterile! She'll never have children of her own!"

"Shelley, if I could just explain—" Jax argued.

"Don't speak to me! Don't speak to Karen! Don't go near her. In fact, don't ever speak to her again!" Flustered, she yanked the sleeve of her blue coat back to look at her watch. She sighed. "I need to go pick up Peter and take him to school. But I mean it, Jax. Don't you go near her!" She turned quickly and nearly blundered into Connor, who had quietly approached in the hallway. Grunting, Karen's mother Shelley Lassiter stepped around him and hurried off down the hall, across the lobby, and out the glass double doors.

Connor stared at Jax, who looked like the air had been let out of him. "What the heck? What are you doing here? Who *was* that?" he asked.

Jax stood very still, his eyes moist, his shoulders sagging. "That was Karen's mom," he said quietly. "Karen's here. I had to call an ambulance and bring her in last night."

"*What?* Jax, what happened?" Connor reached out and put his hand on his friend's shoulder. To his surprise, Jax shrugged ever so slightly and away from him, and Connor's hand slid off. Connor cleared his throat and stuck his hands in his pockets. "Come on, man, come and sit down. You look exhausted."

They sat in the plastic chairs in the lobby, and Jax told him the whole story—about the guy at the party and going with Karen to the women's health clinic. "Karen was insistent; she never wanted me to tell anyone. She *specifically* said she didn't want her mom knowing," Jax explained.

"It's okay, Jax. You were trying to protect her," Connor said, nodding.

Jax continued. "I don't know exactly what went wrong with the abortion, but apparently she had a perforation or something? It tore a hole in her womb, I think. They said she nearly died. I went over to her house last night and she was collapsed on the floor and bleeding. She hardly recognized me," he said, shaking his head. He leaned over in his chair and rested his forehead in his hands. He was physically and mentally exhausted.

"Ohmigod, Jax. That's horrible! But she's gonna be okay, right?" Connor asked hopefully.

Jax nodded. "But she won't ever have children. They had to operate," he said grimly.

Connor's mouth fell open in shock. For a moment, he had no idea what to say. "Um, it wasn't *you,* was it? You know…" he began.

Jax sat up and looked directly at him, his eyes bloodshot. He looked as if he hadn't slept in a long time. "No, it was *not me.* For the tenth time, I did not get her pregnant!" he snapped. He jumped to his feet and ran his hands restlessly through his curly hair.

"Okay, I'm sorry," Connor apologized quickly.

"The guy who knocked her up is *gone*—completely out of the picture. I thought I would be a good friend and stand by her—going with her to the clinic and all of that—and now everybody seems to be mad at *me!*" Jax exclaimed. *Including Karen.* But he couldn't bring himself to open that painful door. "I just spent half an hour explaining to my dad that I did *not do this*. I told him that I respected Karen's need for privacy. She didn't want me to tell anyone! And her mother—well, you heard what she said to me…"

"That was harsh," Connor whispered.

A thought suddenly occurred to Jax and his eyes opened wide. "Well, what the hell are *you* doing here, if you didn't know about Karen?" he asked, confused.

Connor sighed heavily. "It's Andy. He's in the emergency room. He was pulled out of a burning house, and they won't let me see him," he said.

"*What?* You're kidding!" Jax cried. He sat back down. He couldn't take anymore drama in one night.

Connor shook his head. "I was there. The house was over on Baker Street, not far from my place, and my landlord and I walked over there. You know that house, where what's-his-name lives? Andy's friend, um, Will, I think? He's always going over there to watch football—" he tried to explain.

"Yes, I know Will, kind of," Jax said, nodding.

"Yeah, well, the whole house went up in flames, and Andy's been arrested. He's being treated for smoke inhalation, and they have him on suspicion of arson. That's why they won't let anyone see him," Connor finished.

"Arson? *Andy?* Why would they think such a thing?" Jax wondered.

Connor looked up at Jax, his eyes full of pain and confusion. "Jax, you should have seen him. I could hardly believe my own eyes—he was *insane*. He was fighting and thrashing and yelling and throwing those cops around like they were ragdolls!"

Jax sat back down in one of the plastic chairs. "He must've been in shock or something—you know, from all that smoke? He must've been in some state of panic. Maybe he didn't know what he was doing," he suggested.

Connor shook his head again. "I heard the cops talking. They've seen this before—they called it *stacking*. They said he's been doing steroids and I don't know, other stuff, but it's really messed him up," he said quietly.

Jax couldn't believe it. *Andy?* "Well, he'll be okay, won't he? Once he's, you know, over the smoke thing?" he asked hopefully.

"They say they're transferring him to the psych ward. They say he's gone psycho," Connor said worriedly. The images of Andy struggling on the pavement with the police officers haunted him, but even more disturbing had been Andy's chest when they turned him over. His body had completely transformed.

"He's—what? *Andy?* This is so crazy! Where's Simone? Does she know about all this? Did she know he was on steroids?" Jax cried.

"That reminds me! May I borrow your cell phone? I left her a message last night to come down here, but I'll call her again," Connor said. He thought it was odd that he hadn't heard back from her.

Jax nodded and handed over his phone to Connor made the call. "Oh, there's my dad," Jax said, looking out the lobby windows to the parking lot. "He's taking me to school. Would you like a ride?"

"Oh, sure, thanks. Still no answer. I left her another message," Connor said. He quickly punched in another number and waited for a few seconds. *Hmmm. No answer from Celeste either.*

"Maybe we can find her at school," Jax suggested. "My dad said he'll bring me back here to see Karen after school. Maybe she'll be awake then—she's still recovering from surgery now."

"I hope so," Connor said with a sigh. "This is all so weird."

§ § § § §

The weather had turned colder and Connor's lightweight sweatshirt wasn't holding up very well. They had gone directly to school from the hospital so he hadn't had a chance to go home and pick up anything. He decided to go to the shared locker and borrow the red jacket if it was available. He smiled when he saw it hanging there and put it on over his sweatshirt. *Simone must be here if the jacket's here. But why isn't she answering her phone?* Connor wondered.

He didn't have any classes with her until third period. But when he finally did see her, he was surprised to find her sitting all the way in the back of the classroom. She didn't look up when he waved, and he didn't have a chance to talk to her until class ended at 10:45 A.M.

"Hey, Simone, wait up!" he called out when the bell rang.

They were in the crowded hallway when she turned to look at him. Her usually sparkling eyes were red-rimmed; dark bags under them made her appear tired and sickly. She looked awful, with unwashed hair, no makeup, no jewelry—nothing. *This is strange,* thought Connor, taken aback. *Simone's usually so put together.*

Simone really hadn't wanted to come to school at all today. But she didn't want her mother to have a meltdown either. (She tended to do so any time Simone had the smallest sniffle or headache.) Reluctantly, Simone had dragged herself out of bed and showed up. The scene with her irate mother in the middle of the night—after Simone had come home around 3:30 A.M.—had not been pretty. She couldn't afford to piss off her mother any further.

School officials were on standing orders to call her mother immediately if she was ever absent from her classes; her mother was terrified that Simone would collapse somewhere with seizures again. Even though her new medication was working fine, she'd only had one very small seizure in two years. Basically, hiding out in the utility closet or the girls' locker room was not an option. Simone had showed up for her classes, but could do no more than sit like an inert lump in the very back of the room.

"Hi, Connor," she said with a half smile. *Sorry, buddy. I'm not very perky today.*

"Didn't you get my messages?" Connor asked. He looked terrible, as if he hadn't slept all night. His face was full of anxiety.

"Your messages? Oh…no, I guess not. I seem to have lost my cell phone," Simone said. She began to fidget with a strand of her hair. *It's probably somewhere out in the middle of the woods wherever the empty vodka bottle landed. Or maybe it's on the floor of Andy's car…*

Connor grabbed her by the elbow and speed-walked her to the stairwell.

"Connor, what the heck? Will you *slow down?*" she asked. She let out a dramatic sigh. Simone was cranky and in no mood for any weirdness. *Sorry if you're having problems with your family. Sorry if you're having money troubles. I just can't—*

"Simone, Andy's in the hospital," Connor blurted.

A dark void suddenly opened up all around Simone. Connor's words fell into it and nearly disappeared. *What was that he just said? Andy's in the hospital?*

Simone simply stared at him. Her jaw dropped.

"He was in a fire. The police pulled him out of a burning house, but he—um, well, he attacked them. They've arrested him. He's still at County Hospital," Connor explained.

To his surprise, Simone's knees buckled and she started to slide down the wall of the stairwell. He immediately grabbed her and wrapped her in a bear hug, holding her up on her feet. "Simone? *Simone?* Stay with me here, okay?"

Other students passed by them on their way up and down the stairs. A few stared. Most of them just kept walking to their classes. Connor carefully pulled Simone into the corner, hiding her with the red jacket.

The dark void pulled at Simone; its sinister voice threatened to drown out all else. Her heart raced and she fought a sense of panic, remembering her past all over again—her illness, headaches, catheters, hospital monitors, and her parents, her mother especially, crying and praying and weeping around her hospital bed. *No. I am not going there again. Only one seizure in two years. I'm fine. I will be fine.* She took a deep breath and steadied herself against Connor's shoulder.

"Simone? Are you okay?" he anxiously asked. His eyes were wide open.

She nodded, and looked up at him with a faint smile. "Tell me. What happened? Have you seen him?"

Connor glanced away for a moment. "Yeah, I saw him last night. He was on Baker Street, at the house that caught on fire. I saw him when firefighters were trying to put the fire out," he said. He wasn't able to meet her eyes. He didn't want to have to break the news to her.

Alarms erupted in the pit of her stomach. "And *what?* What happened? You were there? Tell me everything that happened!" Simone demanded. She clutched at his arms, feeling the smooth leather of the red jacket beneath her fingertips.

Andy was on the ground in a desperate fight. Red and blue lights lit up his contorted face while the heat from roaring flames blasted all around them as if from a furnace. He fought ferociously with the police officers on the pavement. He shouted and bellowed—simple primal howls of rage without any recognizable words. His eyes were bulging. His muscles were knotted as tightly as a strung bow. It seemed impossible that he could be so strong and so violent—not her Andy, not her sweet man. They were hurting him. Andy was bleeding from the nose. His lip was split open. But he couldn't stop. His eyes were as blank and distant as a raging bull; in fact, it took four cops to subdue him. The cuffs snapped into place around his wrists, and it was a struggle to hold his feet still to cuff his ankles. Finally, he was loaded onto a stretcher and strapped down. An oxygen mask was held over his mouth and nose. Andy fought and shouted the whole time, coating the inside of the plastic mask with a fine spray of blood.

Simone pulled away from Connor and looked up at him in horror. "No!" she whispered. Her throat choked up and tears welled in her eyes.

Connor took her by the shoulders. "Simone, you saw something. What was it? What did you see?" he asked.

"Andy, no, not Andy! Ohmigod, I'm so sorry…I'm sorry…Not you, Andy," Simone dissolved into sobs and Connor held her close.

"Is everything okay?" a voice called out. Connor and Simone turned to see one of the science teachers hovering on the landing in the stairwell. He had seen Simone sobbing. "Do we need to call somebody?"

"She's okay. She's just a little upset," Connor responded. Simone nodded and quickly wiped away her tears.

"I'm okay, Mr. Vander," she managed to get out. "I'm okay, really." She turned and walked down the stairs. Connor followed close behind.

"Simone, what did you see?" Connor persisted, catching up to her, when they were out of sight from everyone.

Simone shook her head fiercely. She quickly wiped the corners of her eyes.

Connor glanced around the hallway on the first floor. Seeing no teachers, he grabbed Simone's arm and pulled her to a stop. "Simone, you need to talk to me! I *know* you saw something!"

"I—I—I guess I saw what you saw!" she finally said, her eyes wide. "Andy was on the pavement. There were lots of police officers everywhere. He was—he was like an animal, Connor. I don't understand. I can't believe it."

Connor nodded. "I know. I was there," he murmured. He glanced down the hallway again and saw two teachers approaching. It was past time for fourth period, and neither he nor Celeste wanted to call attention to themselves.

"We're on our way, Ms. Hagen," he assured the woman walking toward them with a fake smile. "Come on, Simone." Still holding her elbow, he leaned down and whispered as they headed to their English class. "Jax's dad is picking him up after school to take him back to the hospital. We can get a ride with them. Meet me on the steps after last period."

DAY FIFTY-NINE, 5:12 P.M.

Andy had been transferred to the psychiatric ward and wasn't allowed to have any visitors. Simone was beside herself when she found out—wild-eyed and tearful in a tailspin of anxiety, panic, and self-recrimination.

"This is all my fault," she muttered for the third time, crossing and uncrossing her arms repeatedly as she paced back and forth in front of the psych ward. "I really have to see him. I have to talk to him."

"Simone, will you please calm down?" Connor asked, getting a little exasperated. "It is *not* your fault! Listen, we've been here for an hour. They're not allowing any visitors in to see him. Let's go over to the North Wing. At least we'll be able to see Karen."

Simone stopped pacing and stared at him in disbelief. "Wait. Karen's *here* in the hospital?" she asked incredulously.

"Yes, I told you everything already. Jax is there now," Connor explained.

Simone blinked, holding back tears. "She had an operation due to a bad abortion," she stated.

"Yes," Connor replied, looking down at the floor.

"And now she'll never have children. And it wasn't Jax who got her..." her voice trailed off.

"*Yes,* Simone. We've been through all of this already. Come on, why don't you sit down for a minute?" Connor suggested. He gingerly put his arm around her shoulders and tried to steer her to a row of plastic seats to rest.

He distinctly heard the creak of a worn wooden step on the side porch of a house. He could see two lovers through a window. They had gone inside after necking on the sofa on the porch. Three lumpy cushions lay on the sofa—a faded red and gold flower print—and a white lacy pair of underwear had been tossed on the middle cushion. An umbrella stand was positioned next to the couch; its two umbrellas leaned against it, along with a single muddy boot that had been there for a long time, and a cardboard box full of old newspapers. Shame, betrayal, grief, outrage—

Simone pulled away from him. "What are you doing?" she whispered. "You're doing something." Her eyes were wary and frightened.

Connor shook himself and blinked. The vision of the wooden porch had been so real, as if he had been standing on the creaky step. He could've reached out and touch the threadbare cushions of the old couch. "Simone, honey. Please just calm down. Let's go see Karen," he suggested.

Simone backed away from him, shaking her head. "You go. I'm staying here. Andy's parents are coming. I have to talk to them. I have to talk to *him*. They're only allowing immediate family members in to see him; I can get them to let me in. I have to talk to him, Connor. You don't understand," she said firmly.

For the tenth time, Connor wished Celeste was here with them so she could stay with Simone. Simone seemed shaky and off-balance. The three of them had formed a little fellowship in his rented room, and he missed her. He needed her. But he'd tried calling her again on the lobby pay phone, and there was still no answer. *Celeste, where the heck are you? I'm worried.*

Connor sighed and nodded. "Come and find me at Karen's room afterwards. It's on the second floor—Room B420 in the North Wing," he said. Simone nodded and watched Connor walk away from her.

§ § § § §

Jax was already there, and Connor found him on the second floor leaning on the wall outside of Karen's room.

"Hey, Jax. How is she?" Connor asked anxiously. "Is Karen awake now?"

Jax looked at Connor for a moment before responding. "She's awake, yes, but her mom is in there now. I can't let her see me. Remember, I'm not supposed to be here," he muttered.

A commotion erupted as Karen's mother emerged from her daughter's room. She was still wearing her blue coat, and she was arguing profusely with the nurse. Jax backed off down the hallway to watch from the corner of the corridor. Connor stood in front of him.

"I need to speak with the doctor right away!" Shelley demanded, her voice edgy and loud. Her hair was uncombed and her eyes were red. "My own daughter doesn't even recognize me! Something is obviously wrong, and nobody will tell me anything! There must be a problem with the anesthesia, or the medication or something."

The nurse tried to calm Shelley down. "Ms. Lassiter, we're doing the best we can…" she began.

Shelley glared at her. "My daughter says her name isn't Karen! She thinks her name is Tess or something!"

"But Ms. Lassiter—" the nurse tried to interject.

"She says I'm not her mother! I need to know what's going on here!" Shelley cried. "What are you people doing about this?"

"Ms. Lassiter, your daughter is in a fugue state," the nurse explained, trying to steer her away from the door. "It's from stress, and it's very important that she not have too much excitement." She glanced at Karen's door and back at Shelley and raised her eyebrows.

"She doesn't even recognize her own mother! You people must've given her the wrong medication or something! I want to see your supervisor *now!*" Shelley barked.

"Right this way, Ms. Lassiter," the nurse shot back. She marched Karen's mother down the hall to the nurse's station.

Connor turned to Jax, confused. "A fugue state? What the heck is that?"

Jax's eyes were haunted. "I guess it's like she…lost herself, I think. She's having some kind of a psychotic episode. My dad was there when the doctor came earlier. He says he thinks it's temporary, but he doesn't know how long it will last."

"He doesn't know? How can he not know? She's a strong girl. I mean, she's gonna snap out of it soon, right?" Connor asked. Clearly, he was nervous.

"I looked up fugue states online," Jax answered slowly. His voice was a little unsteady. "It said they can last for a few minutes, a few days, or up to a year. Or sometimes…they don't resolve at all."

Connor stared at him. "A year or not at all?" he exclaimed, shaking his head. "She doesn't recognize her mother. Does she recognize you?"

"Shelley's been in and out and yelling at the nurses. Honestly, I haven't been able to get in there," Jax said. He glanced down the hall at the nurse's station. "I don't see her down there. I think they went off to find the doctor." He looked furtive, afraid he would be kicked out of the hospital at any minute. But he was desperate to talk to Karen and make sure she was okay. And find out if he was still in the dog-house.

"Jax, buddy, I'm so sorry. This all just sucks," Connor said. He stepped forward and embraced Jax. *The poor guy looks like he could use a hug right now,* he thought.

To Connor's amazement, Jax pulled back as if he'd been struck with a hot iron. "Will you *stop* that?" Jax hissed through clenched teeth. His eyes began to blaze.

Connor stepped back quickly, stunned by the ferocity of his friend's response. This was a Jax he had never seen. "I—I'm sorry, Jax. I didn't mean to—" he stammered.

"I just don't—please just…" Jax said with a tired sigh. He held his hands, palms up, out in front of him. His face was a war zone of emotions. He hadn't intended to hurt Connor's feelings, but it had been a gut reaction. It all just kind of made Jax uncomfortable—the way Connor looked at him, the way he moved, how he wanted to touch him and be close. He didn't want Connor to cross boundaries that Jax wanted to keep intact.

Jax took a deep breath and lowered his hands to his sides, slowly letting the air out through tense lips. "Personal space, dude," he said quietly. His eyes were aloof; the warmth was long gone. "That's all I'm saying. I just need a little personal space."

"No problem," Connor answered quickly, taking another step back. His face was flushed, his heart galloping. *I can't believe this! He's looking at me like I'm some…like he's afraid…In fact, he's been a little standoffish ever since I told him. I didn't expect this of him—not Jax. He's so easygoing, so laidback. I thought he was open-minded. Now he seems almost as homophobic as my dad.* He shuddered at the thought of his dad's face angry face.

Another thought occurred to Connor, and he glanced down at his sleeves. *Did Jax see something when the red jacket touched him?* Embarrassment flooded through Connor's entire body. *No, that's impossible. My thoughts and fantasies are my own business. He can't know…*

Suddenly, he felt like taking the jacket off—and never putting it back on. But he couldn't do that. Another part of him wanted to keep wearing it forever. Besides, it looked good on him, and he didn't have very many possessions anymore.

"Sorry, Jax. I really didn't mean anything," he mumbled, glancing down at the floor. For a moment, he was afraid to look Jax in the face again. He was afraid to see rejection, or disgust, in his friend's eyes. But when he finally did look up, there was only distance. He also noticed a guarded look in Jax's unusual greenish-golden eyes. A pang of regret struck Connor through the heart as he wondered what those eyes would look like filled with love and desire.

Jax turned and walked toward Karen's hospital room.

"Do you mind if I come inside with you?" Connor asked him. Jax shrugged and didn't answer. Connor ignored the tears stinging the back of his eyes as he followed him in.

§ § § § §

Jax was shocked by how pale she looked. "Karen? Karen, it's me, Jax," he said softly. He sat down in the chair by the bed, recently vacated by her mother. There seemed to be no color in her face at all, and her reddish-brown hair stuck to her neck in lank ribbons. An IV line was taped in loops to the back of one hand, and a monitor above the bed whirred and beeped quietly.

Connor hovered at the other side of the bed. "Hey, chiquita. I'm here, too. It's Connor," he said warmly.

Karen stirred and opened her eyes, but only halfway. It was hard to tell if she was really awake.

"Hey, honey," Connor murmured. He gently picked up Karen's hand and cradled it in his own. He made sure to be careful to avoid the tape and plastic lines. The cuff of the jacket brushed against her wrist.

Tess and Jax are getting off a plane with their two children: two honey-skinned imps with masses of curly sienna-brown hair. Tess suddenly laughs and says to her husband, "Have you ever seen so much rain in your life?" Jax laughs, too, and shakes his head in disbelief. As they make their way through the covered terminal walkway, the deafening rainfall fills the air like a solid wall of sound and water.

"Hilo has the most rain of any city in the whole country," Harper reminds them. "I read it online." Their first-born son is nine years old; he's also their resident expert on the Internet.

"Thanks, Harper," Jax says ruefully. "I had heard that Hawaii never gets rain."

Tess grins at her curly-haired family; in this powerful humidity, the curls have all turned into riots of ringlets. She thinks they all look like tropical Raggedy Ann and Raggedy Andy dolls. Just the sight of her family is enough to make her heart burst; they're all so beautiful.

The gray rain, indistinguishable from the earth and the sky, suddenly light up with a preternatural glow. A moment later, it seems as if the whole world has cracked in two. A mighty roar of thunder resonates in their very bones.

Their young daughter looks around in terror, uncomprehending. She wonders if the building is falling down. Has there been an explosion? She clutches at her father's legs so he can't keep walking.

"Thunder immediately after lightning means the storm is right on top of us," announces Harper. "That was on Weatherbee.com."

"Okay, okay, Harper. Thanks for the info," Jax says to his son. He gives him a please-don't-scare-your-sister look, and picks up his little girl. "It's okay, Keisha. It's just thunder. It's loud though, isn't it? But it doesn't hurt anything. It just stays up there in the sky."

Tess watches as their five-year-old snuggles into Jax's shoulder as she always does. Her small arms wrap around his neck. He's magic with those kids. He's their prince, their champion, and their best buddy all in one.

"But lightning comes down, you know," Harper goes on. Apparently, he didn't see the look Jax gave him. "Lightning can strike the ground with fifty thousand volts and leave a crater the size of a swimming pool!"

Keisha started to cry when she hears this new tidbit of information.

"Harper, let's talk about something else, okay?" Tess gently chides him. "You can tell me all about it later—when Keisha's asleep."

Inevitably, they get soaked getting everyone into the taxi. All of their rain gear had been packed in the bottom of their luggage. Tess hadn't realized they would need all of itas soon as they got off the plane. Excited, she tries looking out the car window to get a glimpse of their new home, but only sees rain. The taxi swerves and splashes through giant puddles; more water pounds against the windshield. The frantic windshield wipers have no effect at all, but the driver doesn't seem to mind. He drives confidently, even though the road is hardly visible directly in front of the car.

Hilo, on the Big Island of Hawaii, will be their home for the next eighteen months. They had been planning this move for two years, after their stay in Central America, and a year in the Balkans before that. Jax has a Fulbright Fellowship to study the ethnomusicology of Polynesian stringed instruments; Tess will be teaching creative writing as a guest lecturer at the University of Hawaii. Their rented house will be ready in a week, but for now they will be staying in a hotel in Hilo. The house was supposed to have a separate office for Tess, for writing her third novel. She has already sent the first three chapters to her agent. Jax had seen the house on his trip two months previously, and assured her that she would love it. He tells her that it is blue; it's up on stilts; and it has a cupola on top.

It doesn't matter to Tess what the house looks like; she's the luckiest woman in the world. Once she and her family are ensconced within, it will be their home. They had lived in a small apartment in a lively neighborhood in the Balkans, and Harper had played in the streets with all the other children. In Belize, they had lived on a biology research station in the rainforest, and every day they had gone to visit the bird lady down the road. Her job it was to raise orphaned baby parrots and howler monkeys, and then release them into the jungle. They'd gone on night expeditions with her in her Land Rover, and Keisha loved the bush babies with their large, luminous eyes. Twice, they had seen a wild jaguar on the night drives, and Harper had recited a whole encyclopedia entry about their natural history.

Tess has been a news correspondent for the American Embassy. She has also written her second book. Jax spent every free moment learning African drumming while they were in Belize. There were several drumming groups in the villages near the research station; they would all come together for friendly competitions around a bonfire. They'd indulge in local food and dance and spend time with good neighbors under the star-filled sky. In fact, now Harper was a better drummer than his father. Jax would hold baby Keisha until she soon fell asleep to the pounding of drums so often that it was still the best way to get her to sleep. Their friends and neighbors had cried when the Montclairs had left to return to the States, but Tess's contract was up and Jax had to finish his Master's degree.

Rain drips through the windows of their Hilo hotel room, so they pull the beds away from the windows and try stuffing towels along the sills. Finally, the kids fall asleep in one double-bed—perhaps the pounding of the rain reminded them of drums. Jax and Tess snuggle into each other's arms in the other bed.

Tess smiles into her husband's neck, feeling the warmth of her own breath. He always knows when she's smiling. He always wants to know from whence it came.

"What are you thinking about?" he whispers into her ear. Tess is their keeper of sweet memories. Sharing them makes Jax smile, too.

"Keisha. Remember when she was born?" Tess replies softly.

"Ah, well, no. To be honest, I seem to have forgotten all about that," he quietly admits. It had been one of the most stressful experiences of his life, and his wife absolutely delighted in recounting every excruciating detail. Not so much the birth itself, but Jax's unexpected and, well, terrifying role. How he loved to be reminded of what a doofus he had been.

"Really? Well, lucky for you, I remember it very well," Tess giggles into his shoulder.

"I'm sure you do," he smiles.

"I remember telling someone—maybe it was you—that I was having contractions and we should go to the hospital," she explains.

"Oh, really?" he asks, interested in her memory. He enjoys when his wife pokes fun at him.

"And I remember someone—I'm pretty sure it was you—saying, 'Oh, no. Don't be silly! We have plenty of time still. There's no need to rush off to the hospital just yet,'" Tess whispers.

"I can't imagine ever saying that," Jax kids.

"I remember this one guy sitting there, telling me, 'Remember how we spent sixteen hours at the hospital when Harper was born? We don't need to do that again. We might as well be comfortable at home and then go in later,'" Tess continues.

"That guy must've been an idiot," Jax muses.

"I remember thinking, Hmmm, that's odd. It seems like when a pregnant woman says she needs to go to the hospital, maybe somebody should listen. *But I guess somebody was already an expert on birthin' babies, since he'd seen it once, at the hospital, done by experts," Tess says. She begins to giggle again.*

"Well, what more does that somebody need?" Jax asks.

Tess can hardly muffle her giggles at this point. "So that somebody ended up having to deliver his own daughter, at home, on the floor, with his bare hands! It was approximately half an hour after his wife said it was time to go to the hospital!" Her shoulders are shaking with laughter as she buries her face in his chest. The effect is contagious as if she can infect him with her mirth. She always does this to him—especially with this story. It was one that they took out and gently plucked apart on a regular basis, passing it back and forth like a glass of fine wine. Jax always jokes about what an idiot he had been for not listening to her, but Tess always admits that she thought he was really a hero at the time.

For a moment, they rock with silent laughter, trying not to wake up their kids. They hold on to each other and enjoy their moment of deep togetherness—of sharing something no one else has.

Finally, the laughter wears itself out and they lay in sweet silence. The rain caresses the rooftop above the happy couple.

"I will never forget that feeling," Jax murmurs quietly, right before falling asleep. "The feeling of holding Keisha in my hands, right after she was born. One minute she was sleeping, like in a dream, and the next moment she came to life. Right in my own hands. Just like that." Even after all these years, he's still amazed by the experience.

"Just like that," Tess murmurs back. "Yes, just like that."

§ § § § § §

Connor stared at Jax, and then looked back at Karen's face. Her eyes were closed as if she were asleep. Her eyelids fluttered ever so subtly. *That's incredible—is it real?* He had just looked in on someone else's life—or the future of someone else's life. He wasn't quite sure. Carefully, he let go of her hand. *Was all of that really just a dream? Is it possible that Karen still could have children someday?*

Jax was staring back at Connor. *What the heck? Is something wrong? Why does he have that goofy look on his face?*

"I—I think Karen has…gone somewhere, for a while. I think she's currently in a place where she's happy. I think you might want to see it," Connor whispered to him urgently.

"I should see it? What are you talking about?" Jax asked cautiously.

"Well, I know it sounds crazy, but I *saw* something. I saw…what she sees. I think I saw what she's dreaming," Connor tried to explain. He picked up Karen's hand again with his right hand. He reached his left hand across the bed to Jax. "If you just take my hand, then maybe…"

Jax stared at him, his golden eyes hard and glossy. He glanced down at the offered hand but made no move to take it. *Ugh. Hadn't he listened to what I said earlier?*

"Come on, Jax, just do it—" Connor urged.

The door to the hospital room burst open, and Shelley Lassiter marched in with a nurse and a police officer. "Jaxon Montclair!" Shelley announced, pointing a manicured finger at Jax. "Officer, please arrest this boy! He is not allowed anywhere near my daughter."

"Ms. Lassiter, as I explained, you need a restraining order, and you don't—" began the officer. He was clearly irritated by her. Shelley cut him off.

"Then I'll get one, but I want him out this instant! He nearly got my daughter killed. I want him out!" she demanded. Then she turned to the nurse. "This guy is not allowed in here! Do you understand?"

"Ms. Lassiter, we can have you removed as well," the nurse warned. "Your daughter is supposed to have quiet and no stress. You are disturbing her."

"She's my daughter! I am not disturbing her!" Shelley argued.

Tears were rolling down Karen's pale face, and still she kept her eyes closed. They were all pulling her away—taking her away from Tess and Jax, taking away from her real life, the one she was meant to have. Connor leaned forward and kissed her cheek. "We'll be back later, okay, honey?" he promised.

"Okay, I'm going to have to ask all of you to step out," the police officer announced. He put his hands on his hips.

Jax opened his mouth to protest, but Connor grabbed his arm. "We were just going, officer," he said, smiling politely.

Shelley Lassiter headed back toward the nurse's station to speak with the supervisor; Connor and Jax were escorted out to the parking lot.

"If you return and she does have a restraining order," the police officer explained to Jax, "I will have to arrest you. So just stay away and keep out of trouble. Okay, boys?" He looked sternly at Jax first, and then looked over at Connor. They both nodded and walked away. The cop went back inside the hospital.

"I can't believe that witch!" exclaimed Connor as they walked across the parking lot. "A restraining order? For *what?* For you going over to their house, finding Karen bleeding to death, and calling an ambulance for help? Has Karen's mom forgotten about *that?*"

Jax ran his hands through his hair, a habit he had when he was agitated. "I haven't done anything! Like I said, nobody seems to believe me!"

The two boys walked in silence for a few minutes until something suddenly dawned on Connor. "Just be cool, and come with me. I have a brilliant idea…"

DAY FIFTY-NINE, 5:52 P.M.

Connor knew the way to the psych ward in the West Wing; he had spent the wee hours of the morning there waiting—unsuccessfully—to see Andy. "Simone's still there," he said over his shoulder to Jax as they hurried up the stairs and along the corridors. "We can get her to come back with us to Karen's room. Hopefully Celeste can meet up with us, too, if I could just get in touch with her. You haven't gotten any messages from her, have you? The last time I called her, I left your number on her voicemail."

Jax shook his head. "I haven't heard anything from her," he said, slowing down. He stopped and leaned against the wall. He looked frustrated, confused.

"Come on, Jax. What are you waiting for?" Connor asked.

"That's just it, Connor. I don't know. What *am* I waiting for? What's your great idea? Andy's not allowed to have any visitors, and I'm not allowed back in to see Karen. Karen doesn't even want me around," Jax muttered. "So, you tell me—what am I waiting for? Honestly, I think I should just go on home."

Jax figured being at the hospital was pointless and a waste of time. Besides, he had other things on his mind. *I should go see Jasmine. I want things to be back to the way they were. I want to be back to the way we were. I don't even care about infections and ex-boyfriends. We'll work it out. I just don't see the point of me hanging around here. No one seems to want me here.* The memory of Jasmine—of Jax and Jasmine before things had crumbled apart—held him in a powerful grip. He was sure that now that some time had passed, she would be so glad to see him and have him back. They would be even better together this time. Jax had more than enough love and desire for both of them; he would make it work. She had to give him another chance. What they had before had felt so right.

"Jax, don't go!" Connor begged. He seemed so earnest, so insistent. "I really think—I just think we should get you back in to see Karen. You didn't even have a chance to talk to her, and I think—no, I *know* she needs you. She needs to talk to you."

He had to suppress his urge to reach out and take Jax by the shoulders. *What should I tell him? How much should I tell him?* Connor hesitated, unsure of how to describe the vision he had experienced, but he knew it was important. He also felt that if Jax left now, without ever having a chance to connect with Karen, something would be lost forever. Somehow, he knew the paths they all would take during these strangely turbulent times would not be able to be retraced later.

Had he seen the future? But it was an impossible one, if that's what it was. Karen was never having children of her own. Somehow he must have tapped into Karen's dreams of possibilities. The memory still made Connor feel a little embarrassed, as if he had been present on someone's wedding night. He shouldn't have been there; he shouldn't have seen what was hers to see.

Jax, you have no idea how much this girl loves you, Connor wanted to explain to his friend. *It's something rare and special. What I saw— what I felt—was the kind of love some people spend their whole lives looking for and never find. It was the kind of love I hope to find someday.*

But as Connor tried to find the words to explain all of this to Jax, he knew at the same time that it was unexplainable. That this was something a person had to know and feel on his or her own. If only he could get Jax and Karen together again while she was in this fugue state—before Jax retreated and before the opportunity was lost.

Connor took a deep breath and concentrated on the words he was about to say. "Jax, I know you're feeling bad. Honestly, I do. But please believe me when I tell you that you really, *really* need to see Karen now—today. You must see her as soon as possible. Whatever has gone down with you guys before this, don't worry about it. Right now, she needs you," he said firmly. "*Please,* Jax."

Jax didn't answer. He gazed steadily at Connor, his face guarded, but Connor could see confusion and agony under the surface. He thought he was getting through to him. Jax was beginning to understand the magnitude of the situation.

Connor pressed on. "I thought if we could go find Simone at the psych ward, and maybe find Celeste, too, we could take them over to see Karen. If the two girls go in first, we can wait around the corner and watch for when the nurses aren't looking, then slip in. The girls will be our cover; I'll watch the door. If anyone comes back—the nurses or Karen's mom—you can and I can zip into the bathroom," he said. There was excitement in his voice.

Jax hesitated for a minute. Finally, he nodded. "All right, we'll try it. If we can't find the girls, or this doesn't work, then I'm going, okay?" *And I'll head straight over to Jasmine's place to work things out with her.* Suddenly, seeing Jasmine seemed like the best way out of all this. The Jasmine in his fantasy was going to welcome him with open arms and realize, when she saw him again, how much she truly loved him.

"Come on!" Connor urged. "We're running out of time!" They hurried along the hallways to the psych ward—two men on a mission to make everything in their lives better again.

When they got there, Simone was gone. The nurse at the station mentioned that her parents had come for her, but that was all. No one was allowed in to see Andy except for immediate family.

"Connor," Jax suddenly whispered urgently, tapping Connor's arm. "That's the same cop over there. Look!"

The police officer who had escorted them out to the parking lot was talking to an orderly with a cart of laundry. He hadn't yet seen Jax and Connor. If he did see them, and if Karen's mother had a restraining order, Jax would get arrested on the spot.

Jax turned and pushed back through the double doors. "Sorry, Connor. I have to get out of here. Don't be mad; I tried. I'm going home!" he exclaimed in a low voice. He didn't want the cop to hear him.

"Jax, wait!" Connor hurried after him. "Please, just come back to Karen's room with me. Just for a few minutes. I'll stand and guard the door. I'll let you know if anyone comes. Don't you want to at least talk to her?"

Jax hesitated again. "Dude, I don't want to get arrested!" he cried. Connor just stared at him with pleading eyes. Jax sighed and smacked his own forehead. "Of course I want to talk to her," he admitted. "But I can only go in for a few minutes. You better keep a close eye on the hallway. The second someone starts heading in our direction, I'm out of there. Got it?"

Connor grinned. "You bet."

They took the elevator down and crossed back over to the North Wing. They passed the emergency area on the way over. A cluster of people crowded around a gurney with a small, blanket-covered figure strapped to it.

Connor's pace slowed as something caught his eye.

"What's the matter?" Jax asked. "Why are you slowing down?" He followed Connor's gaze to an Asian family milling about in the hallway.

Without warning, Connor sprinted down the hall to the cluster of people just as the gurney was wheeled through opaque double doors. "*Wait!* Celeste! Mrs. Nguyen!" Panic colored his voice. Jax realized who was on the gurney and hurried after Connor.

Two male members of the family stepped in front of a weeping woman, shielding her from Connor's wild-eyed approach. One of them, a neatly groomed man of about forty years, held his hand up. "Please, Connor. Please, excuse us during this time," he said blankly.

"Mr. Nguyen—you're her uncle, right? Was that her? That wasn't Celeste, was it?" Connor asked, terrified. He craned his neck to look through the double doors that had just swung shut

"Celeste is ill, Connor," he said gravely. "It's not good."

"*What?* What's the matter with her? I have to see her!" he cried.

Celeste's uncle firmly took Connor by the elbow and quietly steered him away from the weeping woman. She must've been Celeste's mother.

"Connor, this is a private family matter. There is nothing you can do. Please go," he asked.

"But I have to see her! I'm her best friend, Mr. Nguyen. You *know* she would want to see me," Connor begged. His words were intense and insistent.

A look of pain crossed Mr. Nguyen's face. "Yes, Connor, I know. But she cannot see anyone now. Celeste is in a coma," he said. With that, he turned and walked back over to comfort Celeste's mother.

§ § § § §

Jax steered Connor to another molded plastic chair and sat him down carefully. "Connor, breathe. What did he mean when he said she was in a coma?" he asked. "He means some kind of temporary thing, right? Maybe she fell and hit her head or something…"

Connor felt like he was in a coma himself. "I don't know," he whispered. "I don't know. He just said nothing like this had ever happened in their family before. He said he wishes they had sent her back to Vietnam to live with her aunt—before any of this happened."

"Before any of *what* happened?" Jax asked, confused. "And wasn't she born here in America? What does he mean?"

"A drug overdose," Connor whispered, shaking his head slowly from side to side. His eyes looked like they were going to spill over with tears. "They say it was a drug overdose. Her family doesn't want me to talk about it. They're very private, but…because I'm Celeste's friend, because…" He dropped his face into his hands and began to sob. "Ohmigod, Celeste!"

Jax shifted uncomfortably from foot to foot, uncertain how to comfort Connor, who was clearly in pain. "I'm…sorry, Connor. I'm really sorry about Celeste. I know how much she means to you," he said. He awkwardly put his hands out to comfort his friend, but quickly put them down at his sides again. There was no response from Connor.

Jax took a few steps away. "I guess, um, I'll go now. I mean, if you want to, you know, be alone, I completely understand…" he stammered.

Connor jumped up from the chair, startling Jax. "No! Don't go!" he cried, grabbing Jax by the wrist. "You're coming with me! We're going to see Karen!" Jax was too shocked to reply as Connor dragged him away from the emergency area and back to the North Wing.

§ § § § §

They paused at the corner where the two hallways met to scout out the corridor outside of Karen's room. Another rolling bed was being wheeled into B-420—a bed with an older gray-haired woman who was hooked up to IVs and heart monitors. Connor glanced around and looked over at a cart that was pushed up against the wall. It was piled high with old newspapers, three vases of flowers, and some used towels. The rooms were being cleaned.

"What are you doing?" Jax whispered as Connor approached the cleaning cart. He had his eye on the flowers. Connor took a handful of the least droopy stems and turned to Jax. "Flowers for Aunt Millie," he said, nodding toward B-420. "You know, Karen's new roommate. I'm going in to visit my Aunt Millie. You're coming with me for moral support."

Jax followed, still wondering what Connor was up to. Why was this so important *now?* He was nervous about running into Shelley again, or a nurse who recognized him, or the police officer who could arrest him. Besides, he didn't even know if Karen *wanted* to see him.

But she definitely did. When they entered her room, her eyes opened as soon as he sat down next to her bed. Her left hand fluttered, as if seeking his to hold it, so he gently did.

Connor hovered behind him, glancing surreptitiously at the chart at the end of the old lady's bed. "Margaret Peterson," he murmured. "Aunt Maggie." Then he wandered to the doorway of the room and pulled the door nearly closed. He stood watch like a hawk, making sure no one was approaching, and then glanced over at Jax.

Jax bent his head close to Karen's face. He looked uncomfortable, like he wasn't sure what to do or say—or expect.

He needs the red jacket! He should be wearing it so he can—But Connor wasn't exactly sure what Jax would be able to do. He just desperately wanted him to see what he had seen—to know what he knew. Everything would make sense then.

And he desperately wanted to get back to Celeste.

"Karen?" Jax whispered softly. "...Tess?"

Karen closed her eyes as tears leaked out, tracking silently across her skin. "It's Karen. At the end of it all, I'm still plain old Karen, nothing more," she muttered. "Just another stupid chick who has stupidly wrecked her life."

Jax hated the dead, resigned quality to her voice. "What do you mean, *wrecked?* You're going to get through this. You'll recover, and life will go on," he insisted. But even as he spoke the words, they sounded cliché.

Karen turned her head back to him, her eyes dull and cynical. "Go on to what? More of the same? I'm a failure, Jax. I'm plain and geeky and I'm never going to amount to anything," she whispered, deflated.

"Tess," Jax whispered urgently. "Stop. Just stop it. Mistakes happen, but it's what you learn and how you deal with these setbacks that really matters. You're stronger than this. I *know* you!" He leaned forward, his expression intense.

"Jax, this is a mistake that can't be undone," Karen moaned, waving her hand nonchalantly over her covered body. Tears welled up in her eyes again. "Who's going to want me now? Face it, Jax. I'm just a failure." She closed her eyes again and exhaled slowly. "Thanks for coming, but you don't have to come back to check up on me." She turned her head away, and pulled her hand out of his.

Jax stared at her in confusion. This was not the friend he'd grown up with. Where was the girl with a smile that could light up the stratosphere? Where was the girl with a million ideas, full of fun and plans and dreams? Where was the girl who looked after her brother *and* her mother, as well as a scared thirteen-year-old in an abortion clinic? Where was the girl who went on a nineteen-mile bike ride with him and painted flowers on his cast when he fell and broke his leg? Where was the girl who listened to his music and smiled and sighed and teared up when it moved her? Where was the girl who knew him like no one else on earth did—not even Jasmine?

And he knew her. This was *not* his best friend. Panic rose in him as he tried to find the words he needed—the words which would snap her out of this. "Boogerhead..."

She didn't open her eyes. "Just go, Jax."

Feeling rejected, he stood up and walked over to Connor, who still stood guard at the door. "Connor, I've never seen her like this," he whispered. "It's like she's *given up* or something. Coming here was a bad idea."

Connor stared at him, his expression challenging. "And what about you?" he asked.

"What do you mean?" Jax asked, his brows knitting together.

"Are *you* giving up on her? Now, when she needs you the most?" Connor asked.

Jax's eyes widened, and then he scowled. "No. No, I'm not giving up," he snapped. "I would never give up on her." He turned quickly to go back to Karen's bedside.

Connor grabbed his elbow. "Wait, you should put this on," he offered. He began to take the red jacket off.

Jax waved him away. "I'm not putting that thing on," he argued. He couldn't stand the memory of Jasmine he had had while wearing it—sick and wasted and reduced to nothing but a shell of herself.

"But Jax..." Connor insisted.

"No!" Jax said firmly, shaking his head. He sat back down next to Karen, and took both of her hands in his own. She looked away but he didn't let it bother him. "Listen, I know you want to be alone, but I'm here. I'm here now and I'm not leaving. I'm sorry I wasn't there when that guy did what he did, or when your stepdad molested you, or when your mom had a nervous breakdown. I wish I could've stopped all those bad things from happening to you. I wish I could cast a spell over you so you would never suffer again—so no harm would ever come to you," he said. He felt a wave of emotion come over him, and he tried to keep his composure. He had to be strong for the both of them.

He continued. "I can't do that, but there is something that I *can* do. Terrible things happen, Karen, but we get through them. You'll get through them, and you'll go on to live the life you want. You just need strength, and you're one of the strongest people I've ever known," he said with a genuine smile. "You're much stronger than I'll ever be, that's for sure."

Wordlessly, Karen turned her head back to look at him. Tears were still streaming down her cheeks. The sight of her so vulnerable—so exposed as if he were seeing into her very core—awakened something from deep within.

"Karen, I once went rafting on a river, remember?" Jax's eyes locked with hers and his voice took on a hypnotic quality. "The water was deep, and swift, and unpredictable, and the rapids were *unbelievable*. The raft overturned, and I was thrown into the middle of it all. I thought I could keep swimming and get to the riverbank, but it was in a canyon and the sides were steep and rocky. The current was so violent that I couldn't keep my head above the water. I exhausted myself as I attempted to swim through three runs of rapids. Soon, I felt myself starting to sink—starting to black out. I could hear more thrashing water up ahead, and knew I'd never survive a fourth run of rapids. I was drowning. Suddenly, I understood how people drown even when they were good swimmers. I knew I was going to die."

He paused a moment, making sure that Karen was really listening to him. She was. He squeezed her hands and continued. "I didn't want to die. I wasn't ready, and I wasn't going to give up. All I could think about was that I would never see you again. I just kept thinking how sad you would be if I died. I made a decision then and there that I *needed* to get out of the water so that I could see you again. Somehow, I remembered that water rushing around a rock will create an eddy in front of it. I thought I was finished, that I had no more strength to swim, but I reached down deep and managed to get myself over to a big rock in the river. The eddy in front of it held me up. It held me against the rock and kept me from getting swept downstream."

That's how I feel now, Karen thought. *But I feel like I already drowned. Now, I'm just floating along. My life is over.*

Jax could tell Karen was comparing his near-death experience to her current state. He hoped she would continue listening until he made his point. "I didn't have the strength to climb up onto the rock, but I rested there—in that eddy, that quiet spot—and was able to breathe again. Eventually, I gained enough strength to climb up onto the rock, and that's where I waited. That's where my dad and the other guys found me when they came downriver in the boat, and picked me up. I never said anything. I never told anyone how close I'd come to drowning. But you were there with me the whole time, Karen. I don't know that I'd have been able to find the strength to keep fighting if it hadn't been for you—if it hadn't been for the thought of never seeing you again…"

Why didn't he tell me any of this before? Karen wondered. *And why is he telling me this story now? He said he only likes me as a friend. Is he trying to make me feel worse? Why is he going out of his way to be so nice?*

"…And now I'm giving it back. You're being swept downstream, and you're in that timeless, endless loop of despair. Now I'm helping you find the quiet spot, so you can recuperate, and I'm reminding you that you have more strength than you think, Boogerhead," Jax grinned.

Karen cracked a small smile. Jax was finally getting through to her.

He leaned in close. His gold-flecked sparkling eyes easily held her gaze in a soft but relentless grip. "You gave me the strength I needed when I thought my life was over. You helped pull me out onto the rock, and now I'm pulling you out. I'm right there with you, Tess. We're sitting on the rock in the river—just breathing and resting—until you're ready to go out again," he said softly.

Karen slowly pulled his hand up to her own face, and rested it against her wet cheek. She sighed, releasing all of her worries and fears. In that moment, Jax felt his world shift. This was his best friend, his confidante, his partner, his love. No one knew him better; no one loved him more. No one would be a more true companion or a better soulmate.

Why didn't I see this before? Where are these feelings coming from? Jax wondered. *And what about Jasmine? Did she really mean that much to me, or was it more about her image and the fact that she was in a band?* The more he thought about it, the more Jax felt his obsession with Jasmine dissolve—breaking up and washing away in Karen's teardrops that rolled down her cheeks.

…Only the girl in front of him wasn't Karen anymore. Karen was the four-year-old who got a jellybean stuck up her nose—the little dorky girl with braids and glasses. This was Tess, *the woman.*

"I love you, Tess," he found himself whispering. His eyes were suddenly misty, and she held his hand tightly against her face. With his other hand, he pulled his cell phone out of his pocket, flipped it open, and reprogrammed one of the names in his address book with his thumb. Smiling, he showed it to Karen.

Instead of BOOGERHEAD, the screen now boldly displayed TESS.

Karen smiled back at him. "Better reprogram that awful ringtone, too," she replied.

Connor suddenly gasped from the doorway. Jax and Karen both looked up, startled. Jax's heart began to beat faster. He wasn't sure if it was because he was afraid of getting arrested or because he just realized how much Karen—Tess—meant to him.

"Simone! Come inside, honey!" he exclaimed, stepping back to open the door wider. "I've been trying to get in touch with you forever!"

Simone burst into the room and threw her arms around Connor. She was sobbing, her hair was a mess, and her face was streaked with tears.

"Simone, what is it? What's the matter?" Connor asked her incredulously. "Are you okay?"

"It's Andy!" she blurted. "He's under arrest. He's being charged with second degree murder!"

DAY FIFTY-NINE, 6:24 P.M.

"What?" Connor exclaimed. "*Second-degree murder?* What are you talking about?"

"The people in the fire—" Simone tried explaining between sobs. "Two of them. Two of the people in the house—"

"They *died?*" Jax cried, horrified.

"What fire? What people?" Karen asked. She was completely out of the loop. "What's going on?"

"The—the people died. Now Andy is—now they've charged him—and he's arrested, and—" Simone clutched at Connor and stared at him. She was hysterical. He had never seen her so worked up before. Her entire face was contorted with fear. "Connor, *Andy didn't do it!* He didn't start the fire!"

Connor embraced her and tried calming her down. "Shhh. Of course he didn't do it, Simone. He would never—" But he suddenly stopped mid-sentence and frowned. *I can see the couch. And there's a white pair of lacy underwear on the cushion, and the box of newspapers...*

Connor took Simone by the shoulders and stared at her, hard. Then he slowly took the jacket off. "Simone, honey, put this on. You need to put this on and see for yourself. You need to know what happened."

Simone cried and sniffled while Connor carefully put the jacket on her, as one would dress a child. Then he wrapped his arms around her and held her close. "It's all right, Simone. I'm right here with you. No matter what, I'm not going anywhere..."

Simone's eyes grew wide with fear, and then clenched tightly shut. A low moan escaped her throat as she saw the events of the night of the fire unfold.

"Jax, Connor—what's going on?" Karen asked, alarmed. Her eyes darted back and forth at the two of them, and then over at Simone, who looked terrified. "What's the matter with Andy? What is Simone seeing?"

Jax murmured quietly to her while Connor held Simone. She was visibly shaking and looked as if she might crumple to the floor if Connor let go.

"Shhh. It's all right," Connor told her, his voice gentle. "You just have to tell them. You have to tell them what happened. Tell them it was an accident. It's okay, Simone. Remember, I'm right here."

Sobs broke loose from Simone as if her heart were trying to burst out of her body. "*No!*" she moaned. "I didn't mean—I never meant—I'm sorry! I'm *so* sorry. Connor, what do I *do?* I had been drinking…"

Jax jumped to his feet as the police burst into the room, thinking they were coming for him. The old woman in the second bed, who had been heavily sedated and sleeping until now, jerked awake and began asking where her son was.

"Ohmigod!" Simone went into hysterics when she saw the officers. She began clawing at Connor to let go of her. Karen and Jax watched in astonishment.

"Simone McTavish, you are under arrest. Anything you say can or may be used against you…" began one of the officers as the other tried to take her away from Connor. With a burst of strength no one expected, Simone broke free of both Connor and the cop. She threw her arms in the air and let out a primal scream which brought frantic footsteps from nurses and security guards into the hallway.

Jax, Karen, and Connor watched the frightening drama unfold. It was as if Simone were in slow motion. Her arms sliced through the air in a graceful ballet. Suddenly, her head flung back and her mouth opened wide. She no longer looked graceful as the floor came up to meet her, welcoming her head with a crack as her body shuddered and pulsed.

None of them had ever seen a grand mal seizure before. Simone looked like a fragile little doll being shaken by a vicious dog, jerking and thrashing and shaking uncontrollably. There was nothing they could do to help.

The hospital staff was swarming the room within seconds: ordering everyone out, protecting Simone's head and neck, getting her onto a gurney, and wheeling her out to some official hospital location. Panic-stricken, Connor took off down the corridor after her. Jax snuck back inside B420 and held Karen in a wordless embrace.

§§§§§

"What are *you* doing in here?" Karen's mother demanded when she saw Jax back in the hospital room with her daughter. They seemed to be *very* close together. "I told you to stay away from her!"

Jax stood up. "She's not in the fugue state anymore," he said quietly.

"I warned you. Now I'm calling the—" Shelley began.

Karen cut her mother off. "It's okay, Mom," she said. She reached for Jax's hand. He cautiously sat back down in the chair by her bed. "Jax isn't going anywhere. He's my best friend, and he saved my life." Karen looked adoringly at him. "More than once."

Shelley was getting herself wound up and red-faced. "But he—" she started.

"Mom, I already told you that it wasn't him. He never told anyone about the abortion because I didn't want him to. You can be mad at me all you want, but you can't blame him. Jax saved my life, Mom. He took care of me," Karen said.

Shelley opened her mouth to say something more, but ultimately dissolved into tears. Jax saw that *this* was really what bothered her— the thought that she somehow *wasn't* taking care of Karen. She didn't like the fact that someone else had been looking out for her own daughter, and not her.

"Mom, it's okay," Karen repeated. "I'm feeling better."

Shelley still stood in the doorway, nearly swaying on her feet. She looked lost.

"I'm getting a little hungry though," Karen said gently. "I think I have the strength now to eat something." She smiled at her mother.

Shelley's reddened eyes looked forlornly at her daughter. "Tapioca?" she asked. She dabbed at her eyes with a tissue she had kept in her coat pocket.

Karen nodded. "That would be great. Maybe there's some down at the cafeteria?" She wanted more alone time with Jax and hoped her mother would take a hint. Shelley did understand what her daughter was trying to do. She nodded, straightened her shoulders, and left the room.

"Robert? Is that you?" a querulous voice called out. It was the old woman in the next bed.

Jax got up. "No, Mrs. Peterson, but look here—someone brought you flowers," he said warmly. Jax picked up the flowers that Connor had dropped and stuck them in tall paper cup. He set the small bouquet on the tray table next to her bed. She smiled.

There was a light knock on the door and Connor entered the room. He was carrying a large paper bag with plastic handles. He set the bag on the floor and slowly sat down in the chair near the door. He lowered himself as if he would never get up out of the chair again. He looked awful.

"Connor!" Karen exclaimed. "What's happening? What's going on?"

"What's happening?" he sighed heavily. There was a tiny bit of sarcasm in his voice as the air rushed out of his lungs through pursed lips. "What's happening with Simone, with Celeste, or with Andy?"

Karen's eyes widened and Jax sat down next to her again. He took her hand. The two of them let Connor catch his breath. They were anxious and afraid, dreading his news.

"Simone," he breathed. He stood up, ran his hands through his hair, and sat back down again. "You know the jacket—the red jacket—and how when you wear it, I mean, when I wear it—"

"You see things," Karen finished for him. "I know. We all know."

"What did you see?" Jax asked him.

"I saw a porch, and a couch, and a lacy pair of underwear. And Simone—I saw her on the porch, looking in the window. She and Andy had had a big fight. I guess they broke up in the process. Simone got drunk, followed him to the house, and saw through the window that Andy was with another girl," Connor explained. "Simone had seen the lacy panties and freaked out. She just meant to make a point, you know, to make a statement by lighting them on fire and having Andy find them. He would then know that she knew what he had done. She was upset. That's why she did it. But she didn't mean to hurt anyone."

"That's why she...?" Jax prompted.

Connor sighed again. His face was infinitely sad. "She set the panties on fire. There was a gas can sitting near the driveway. Apparently, someone from across the street saw her with it. She poured gasoline on the panties, and set them on fire. Then she ran off." He shook his head and continued. "Only they were on the couch, next to the box of newspapers. She was already gone by the time the fire really started going. She didn't see any of it."

Karen looked horrified. "So the house went up in flames? And those people died? What happened to Andy? Was he injured?" she cried.

"He suffered from smoke inhalation. But he went psycho when the firemen tried to get him out of the house, and they had to tackle him and arrest him. He was so crazed that they originally thought he had set the fire, but he didn't. He just went nuts because he's been taking steroids, and some other stuff," Connor shrugged. "It's pretty messed up if you ask me."

"Steroids?" Jax asked. He was surprised. "Where was he getting steroids?"

Connor shrugged. "He probably got them from Will, his buddy who lives in the house. I mean, *lived* in the house."

"Did he—?" asked Karen. Her voice was almost in a whisper. She was shocked by everything that was happening.

"Yes," Connor said, looking down at the floor. "He was one of the ones who died."

"So where is Simone now? Is she all right?" Karen wondered.

"She's in Intensive Care. She had a massive seizure; it took half an hour to get it under control. Her parents are there with her. She's also under arrest. She's being charged with second degree murder. Oh, and Andy's being transferred. They're sending him to some kind of—I don't know—rehab home or something. His parents want to get him clean and sober as soon as possible," Connor replied.

"Ohmigod!" Karen exclaimed, shaking her head. "And I thought *I* was having problems. I had no idea that any of this was going on!"

"And Celeste?" Jax asked him quietly. He looked intently at Connor, trying to read his face without having to hear the painful words.

Connor's eyes brimmed with tears. He struggled to maintain control of his emotions.

"Celeste! What's wrong with Celeste?" Karen demanded.

Connor hung his head. "She's in a coma. She was at a party with that guy—the one she has been dating for a little while now—and they were mixing alcohol and prescription drugs. They've pumped her stomach, but—" his voice trailed off. He looked down at the floor.

"But *what*? She'll be okay, right?" Karen cried. She had put her glasses back on to see better and her eyes were wide with fright.

"They say she might not recover," Connor blurted. Tears dripped down his cheeks. His face turned blotchy. He felt like the room was closing in on him. He took a shallow breath. "They can't say when, or *if*, she'll come back."

The three of them sat for a few moments in shocked silence. A nurse bustled in and out, checking up on Karen's elderly bedside neighbor.

"Wait! I know what we can do," Karen spoke up after the nurse left. "The red jacket! We can use it to our advantage. We can put it on. Perhaps we'll be able to see something about Celeste. Then we'll know for sure…" She leaned forward in her hospital bed, anxious to do something, anything, to help her dear friend.

Connor shook his head. He sniffled a few times and looked away.

"Come on, Connor," Karen urged. "That jacket is something special. We've all felt it; we've all seen things while we've worn it. Some of these visions have turned out to be things that we should've acted on." She looked pensive for a moment, but recovered. "It's like the jacket is some kind of conduit—a clairvoyant door. It's not too late!"

Still, Connor shook his head.

"Where's the jacket, Connor?" Karen persisted. "Weren't you wearing it?"

He reached down and picked up the large paper bag he'd brought in. "It's here. Simone had it on." He set the bag back down and looked vacantly into the hallway.

Jax stood up and walked over to the bag. He reached inside and pulled out a piece of dark reddish leather. "Oh," he said. He looked surprised.

"What? What happened to it?" Karen asked slowly. Jax held up the bag for her to see the jacket for herself. She peered inside to find nothing but a pile of red leather pieces.

"Simone had it on, remember? I wanted her to see what had happened during the night of the fire. I mean, after what I saw, I figured she definitely need to know what happened," Connor said quickly, feeling partially to blame for the demise of the red jacket. "And then she had that terrible seizure. The nurses couldn't get the jacket off of her. Her whole body was convulsing…"

"So they cut the whole thing apart?" Jax asked, stunned.

Connor nodded. "They had to get a vein. They had to give her medication as soon as possible. They destroyed the jacket when they were trying to help her," he said quietly.

A moment passed, and another, as the three friends looked into the bag. Speechless, they just gazed in shock at the shredded jacket—at the shredded lives of their friends.

DAY SIXTY-ONE, 4:20 P.M.

"I can walk, you know," Karen muttered. She looked up at Jax and rolled her eyes. He was wheeling her out of Room B420 in a squeaky wheelchair.

"Hospital regulations," Jax reminded her. "Remember all those discharge forms you had to sign? Just relax and enjoy the ride." He smiled down at her. "Put your seatbelt on!" he joked as he pushed her down the long hallway.

"Be careful, Jax," Shelley warned. She was walking a few yards behind them. In her arms were all of Karen's belongings while she had been in the hospital: her bag, several bouquets of flowers, balloons, and a big teddy bear that donned a surgical cap and mask.

"I will, Shelley," Jax promised. He bent down near Karen's ear. "Think she'd mind if we did a few wheelies?" he whispered.

"I'll go out to the parking garage and bring the car to the front lobby," Shelley said. Her face looked anxious. After everything that had happened, she was afraid to let her daughter out of her sight. She was hesitant about Jax, but she saw how much Karen cared for him; she was making an effort to be nice to him again. He did seem to be very solicitous and responsible. Jax's dad had even had a reassuring talk with her. *He's a good kid,* she told herself.

"Okay, Mom. We'll see you down there!" Karen said. "Remember, we're stopping by to see Celeste for a few minutes first though, okay?"

"Okay, but don't take too long," Shelley responded. "I'll be waiting."

As Jax and Karen waited for the elevator, Jax flipped his cell phone open and secretly dialed Tess. Karen's phone rang, and she suppressed a grin as she answered it.

When she flipped it open, the screen read AZTECA. Boogerhead and Scumbucket had both been retired; the new Tess and Jax were eager to start a new chapter in their lives.

"Why, Jax!" she said with extra enthusiasm into the phone. It was funny to hear her own voice coming out of Jax's phone a few inches behind her. "How nice of you to call!"

"Yo. Wassup? You ready to go home yet or what?" he played along.

"Nah, I think I'll stay here in this fancy hotel," Karen replied. "I can't get enough of the room service or the Jell-O. I absolutely *love* the red kind. And that's all they give me!"

Jax laughed. They walked and rolled in silence through the corridors of the large hospital. "You ready for *this?*" he asked. This time, his voice was quieter. They were getting closer to Celeste's room.

Karen grew silent for a moment. She could feel her throat constrict as it often did when she got nervous or uncomfortable. *Jax, you have no idea. I will never be ready for Celeste in this condition. I don't want to see smart and beautiful Celeste as a vegetable, lying there in a coma. But if it weren't for you, I wouldn't be ready for anything. You have no idea, Jax, what you mean to me. I don't think you'll ever know what having you here with me means...*

But he did. He knew. He snapped his phone shut, and reached forward to close her cell phone, resting his hand on hers for a moment. He kissed her on top of her head.

"I wish I could have seen Simone again, before, you know—and Andy," Karen said. Jax kept pushing the wheelchair along the way.

"I know," he answered. Neither he nor Connor had been able to see Simone or Andy, and now they were out of the hospital. Simone was sent to a juvenile detention center; Andy was now in rehab.

They both heard something as they turned the corner onto Celeste's floor in the South Wing. Karen turned her head to look up at Jax, surprised. *Could it be?*

It was music, a solo violin playing. As they approached Celeste's room, they discovered a crowd of people gathered right outside the open doorway. The song of the violin emerging from the room was exquisite—bittersweet and full of longing. It was a song of love and loss and hopeless dreaming, and Karen's heart threatened to burst as the music filled her.

There was a small rustle as the gathered crowd parted to let Jax and Karen into the room. About a dozen members of Celeste's family were there, along with nurses, and visitors from other rooms. One doctor, two guys who were supposed to be working on the wiring for the lights, and an orderly with a laundry cart were lingering in the room, too. Celeste's uncle ushered everyone into Celeste's room. A hopeful smile was spread across his face this time. Everyone seemed oddly at peace.

Of course, the talented musician was Connor. Jax had recognized his music the moment he had heard it, and he understood the music he was playing for Celeste—a song of pure, unencumbered, unrequited love.

Karen stared in shock at Celeste's small, inert body swathed in blankets on the hospital bed. Her pale face simply looked like she was deep in sleep—unaware of anyone, or anything, and completely unresponsive. *Yes, it's just a deep sleep,* she told herself, trying to make herself feel better. *She'll wake up when she's ready.* She missed her friend tremendously.

She turned to watch Connor play his violin, and the last vestige of control escaped her. She had never seen his face so beautiful, or so filled with pain and desire. Merging and moving with his instrument, his graceful hands caressed the wood and strings and coaxed the music forth as if it came directly from his heart. If these sweet sounds couldn't awaken the sleeping beauty, then nothing would.

Emotion surged like a tidal wave, and Karen found herself dissolving into wracking sobs. She hung onto Jax as if her life depended on it. Jax held her close as they sat together on the rock in the middle of the river. "Remember, I'm here with you," he whispered. "I always will be."

EPILOGUE: DAY 1,826
(Five Years Later)

Karen walked slowly into the visitor's area at the women's penitentiary. There was nothing of beauty in the entire building—not the harsh fluorescent lights in unequal shades of unnatural colors; not the chipped and yellowed linoleum tiles; nor the small, dingy windows changing the sunlight coming through to something lifeless and dull.

The sounds of institutional life jarred and clanged through the sterile hallways: the creak and roll of barred gates being rolled back and then closed again; the snick of locks; the jangle of keys; and the impersonal voice over the intercom. The enormity of the situation—of living for years in such a place—began to sink in on Karen as she waited, trying her best to relax, to act normal, to put on a friendly face. *How on earth can anyone survive in such a place? How can the inmates hold on to their dreams, their loves, or their hopes? This is a real-life hell...*

Karen took a deep breath and closed her eyes. She willed them to stop their stinging. She wished for the memories to retreat back to the distant past—back where they wouldn't overwhelm her.

When she opened her eyes, Simone was there.

The changes were so many, and so profound, that it took Karen a few moments to re-orient herself—to understand what she was seeing. *Long, beautiful hair now replaced by a short, shaggy cut. Cute, chic clothes now turned into a baggy orange jumpsuit with a number on the breast. Glowing, impish expression now replaced by the guarded look of a frightened rabbit. Dreams dancing in her eyes now completely extinguished.*

"Hi, Karen," Simone said. Her voice was, paradoxically, steady and reassuring.

No, that was supposed to be me reassuring you. I'm supposed to be bringing life and courage and the hope of the outside world in with me. But with one look, you can see that I'm weak. Yes, I'm shocked. I need reassuring from you. Some things never change. Karen felt her face flush with embarrassment. "Hi, Simone," she said quietly.

They simply sat for a moment looking at each other.

"You look good," Simone told her. It wasn't a compliment; it was simply as a statement of fact. Karen *did* look good. Her face had cleared up. She had lost twenty pounds. She had traded her glasses in for contact lenses. Her hair was a flattering shoulder-length cut, and she now knew how to control her curls. There were no more frizzy disasters to deal with anymore. The corduroy pants were gone. Instead, they were replaced with black jeans and black suede boots with two-inch heels, making her stand nearly six feet tall. She towered over Jax when she wore her boots, but he loved it; he called her the Amazon Queen.

"So do you!" Karen replied with a little too much enthusiasm. Her words were just a platitude. Karen saw in a moment that truth had a much different place here on the inside. Simone shrugged her shoulders impatiently with the comment. She was no longer concerned with niceties and platitudes. They did her no good here.

"So, how's Jax?" Simone asked curiously.

"He's fine. He's doing fine," Karen answered, relieved to be talking about something else. "He's in school, at a music conservatory. It's on the East Coast, so we don't get to see each other that often since I'm on the West Coast right now. I'm graduating in the spring though. After that, I'll be moving out there. I'm pretty excited…"

"That's nice. Is Jax still playing the guitar?" Simone asked. Karen thought it felt like she was being interviewed for a job.

Where are you, Simone? Are you still in there? Please don't look at me like I'm a friend of your parents, or a kind stranger. "Oh yeah, and piano, and he's writing music. He got together with some friends to record an album, but that didn't work out—artistic differences, you know. But he's reorganizing and plans to do it next summer when we get back from Central America," Karen beamed.

"Oh, that sounds nice," Simone said plainly.

"Yeah, we're spending six weeks in Belize and setting up a little music school there. Jax is friends with a group of drummers who live in a village; we've been there a couple of times already to take drumming lessons from them. They want to start a music school. There are a lot of teenagers from the village who don't have a lot of prospects. There's not a lot of work, and they get into gangs and drugs," Karen explained. "So, the drummers want to teach them music—drumming, keyboards, guitars, and even a choir. I've been raising money and getting donated instruments, and we're taking it all down there this summer."

Karen stopped for a moment, realizing that she was rolling on like a freight train. Simone merely sat there, watching her. *Is she curious? Jealous? Uncomfortable? Does she even care?* It was impossible to tell from her neutral expression. She suddenly felt self-conscious.

"We'll have to see how my high school Spanish holds up through Mexico," Karen laughed nervously. "But they speak English in Belize, so…" She took another deep breath. "Anyway, enough about me! How are *you,* Simone? Are you okay?"

Simone shrugged. "Sure, I'm okay, you know—for someone convicted of second-degree murder who's serving a life sentence. It's about all I can expect, right? I mind my own business. I take my medication. I eat three square meals a day. It's all okay, I suppose," she said nonchalantly. *Except when it's not.* This, Karen could see in her eyes.

"And Andy? Do you ever hear from him?" Karen asked, taking a chance.

Simone struggled for a moment. A flash of emotion spread across her face, but then it disappeared. In that moment, Karen saw an ocean of tears, a sea of grief. "No," Simone finally answered. "He came to see me once about three years ago, and I told him not to come back. He has his own life and I have…this." She leaned forward slightly to the barred windows, the cracked paint, and the buzzing fluorescent lights. "He's doing well, though. He was out of rehab in seven months. He went back to school. He's at some place up north now, studying engineering or something." She smiled a weak smile to let Karen know that she didn't really want to talk about him.

Karen nodded, taking the hint. She hadn't seen Andy since he'd gone to some other school after rehab. His family had moved to a different city. They had said it was for a new start—a better environment. She was glad to hear he was doing well, especially since she had heard various rumors that the effects of the steroids can last years.

"And Connor?" Simone asked curiously. "Have you seen him lately?"

Karen couldn't help remembering Connor in Celeste's hospital room that day, playing the violin for her. She blinked back tears.

"Yeah, I see him periodically. He's living with his boyfriend. He's working full-time and trying to save money for college. He went to a community college part-time for a while, but now he's just working. He's back in touch with his mom, but not his father. He sees her once in a while. He wants to go to art school."

"Good," Simone smiled. "That's good. Art was his thing. I'm glad he didn't give it up."

Karen knew what Simone's next question would be. Before she could ask it, she gave her a brief update on Celeste. "Celeste is at home with her family. It took her almost a year to come out of the coma. She's, um, brain-damaged. I haven't seen her; her family doesn't allow visitors to the house. Connor said she has the mentality of a three-year-old. She hardly talks, and she can't take care of herself. Her mother takes care of her now. I guess that's what she'll be doing for, well, you know…" her voice trailed off.

…The rest of her life. It would've been better if she'd never woken up. It would've been better if we had paid attention to the visions we had. We should've trusted our instincts. If we had taken things seriously when we were wearing that jacket, we could've made different choices. Some of us would be in much happier places right now…

"You're thinking about that jacket, aren't you? That red jacket?" Simone asked, interrupting Karen's thoughts.

Karen looked up, surprised. She nodded. "Yeah, I was. I was thinking that…you know, maybe if we had *listened*—if we had trusted those visions, the things we saw…"

Simone gave a short, mirthless laugh. "And if I hadn't been so drunk, I never would have set those panties on fire. One night of drinking, one huge mistake." *Two people dead, and lifetime in prison.*

Karen nodded. She looked at the neckline of Simone's baggy jumpsuit. It was too big for her; she looked like a child in it. "Do you still have it?" she asked curiously. "You know, the thing Connor gave you?"

Simone nodded and pulled a silver pendant out from under the jumpsuit. It was a necklace with a round silver stud hanging from it. "Yes, see?" she said with a grin.

Connor believed it was the silver studs—not the jacket itself—that were special. After everything had happened, he had taken the red jacket scraps home to his rented room and spent hours removing all the silver studs from the leather: the coverings over the snaps down the front and the ones at the cuffs. He had formed them into unique pendants with silver wire and chains. When he was done creating the necklaces, he gave one to each person in their group of friends—everyone except for Celeste.

Karen reached into her shirt and pulled out her own pendant. She glanced for a moment at the unusual design on it: a tiny coiled serpent with wings. "Celeste's family wouldn't allow visitors anymore, so he couldn't give her hers. He keeps it for her," she explained, examining her pendant. "He thinks she's going to come out of it someday. He thinks that someday he'll put the necklace around her neck and it will ..." her words trailed off. *That it will heal her and bring her back.*

Simone nodded but didn't say anything. She completely understood the power of hope, even though it no longer applied to her. Celeste would never come back, just as she would never get out of prison. But the silver pendant reminded her of hope, and it comforted her to know that four of her friends were living real lives—lives of hope and future and possibility. At first she had been angry and jealous. Now, she simply wished them all well—even Andy. *In the end, everyone is responsible for his or her own actions,* she'd remind herself, especially on days when the confinement became unbearable.

The warden standing at the door signaled Simone and pointed to the clock. Simone put the pendant back inside her collar and stood up.

"Thanks for coming, Karen," she said. "This was fun." She nodded appreciatively for Karen taking the time to visit her, and then disappeared back into the cracked paint and barred corridors.

Karen closed her hand around her own pendant, the winged serpent, and shut her eyes. So much had happened in five years. It was almost too hard too believe. In the end though, she had got what she always wanted: great friends, a good job, and Jax, her soulmate. She thought of her new life—the life she ultimately created for herself—and smiled appreciatively. She let go of her pendant and placed it back in her shirt, against her heart.

It was time to go home.